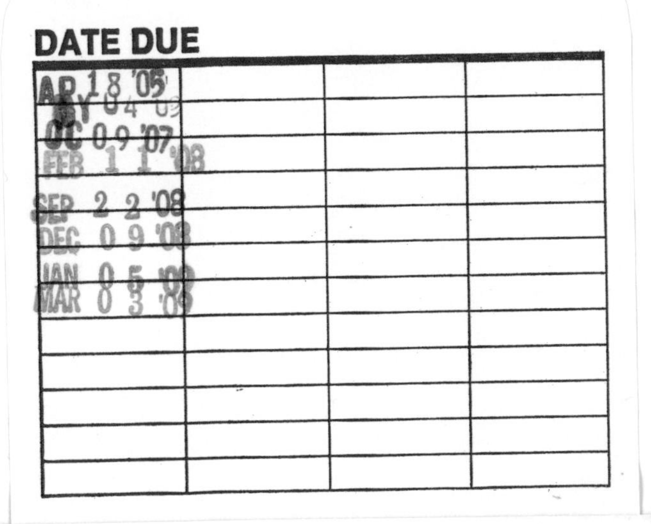

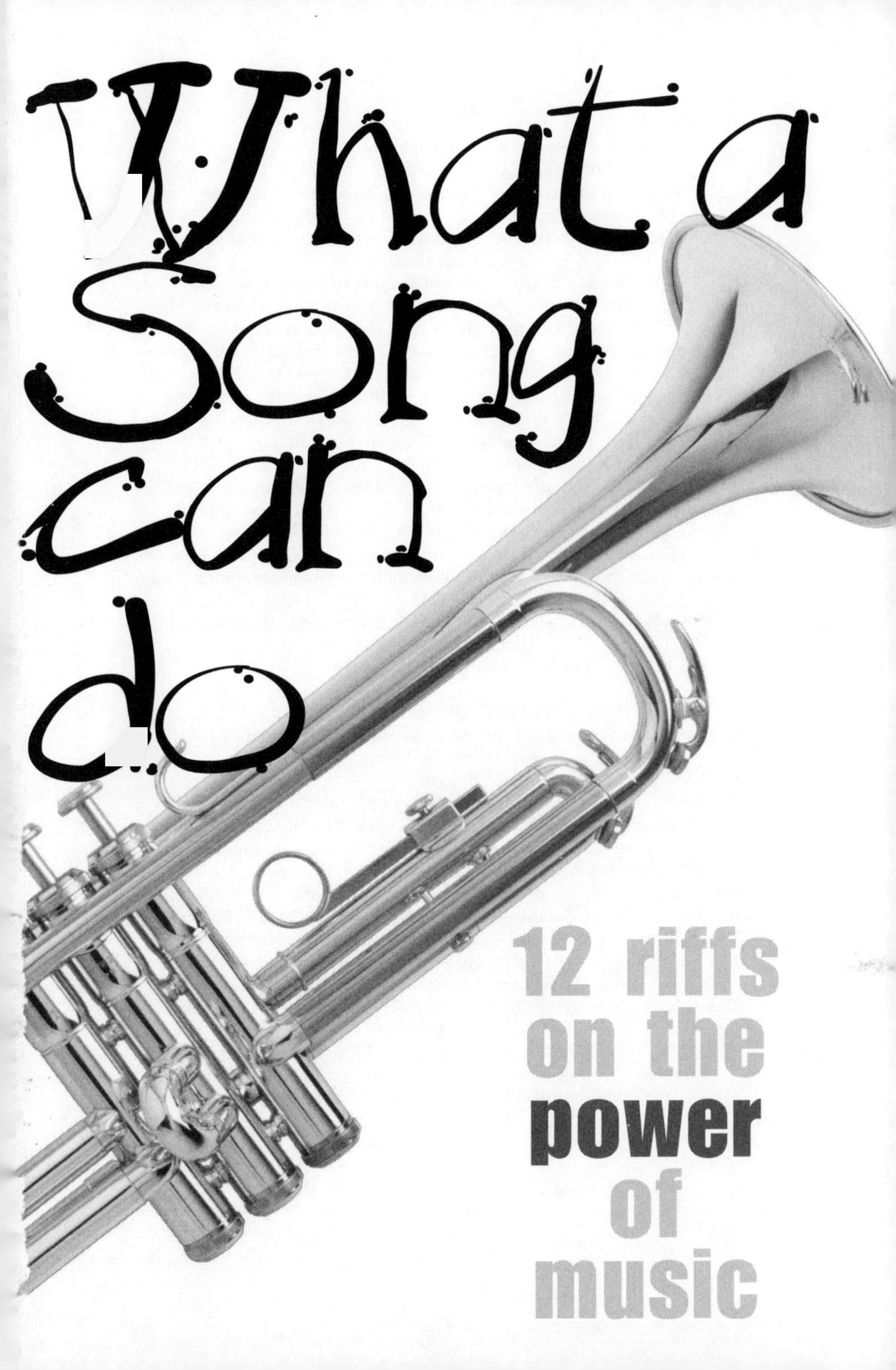
What a Song can do
12 riffs on the power of music

THIS IS A BORZOI BOOK PUBLISHED BY ALFRED A. KNOPF
 Published in the United States of America by Alfred A. Knopf, an imprint of Random House Children's Books, a division of Random House, Inc., New York, and simultaneously in Canada by Random House of Canada Limited, Toronto. Distributed by Random House, Inc., New York.
KNOPF, BORZOI BOOKS, and the colophon are registered trademarks of Random House, Inc.
www.randomhouse.com/teens

Library of Congress Cataloging-in-Publication Data
What a song can do : 12 riffs on the power of music / edited by Jennifer Armstrong. — 1st ed.
p. cm.
SUMMARY: Twelve stories describe the power of music in young people's lives, from forming a community of individuals in a high school band to helping a young man connect to his Indian heritage through ancient songs. Contents: Variations on a theme / by Ron Koertge — A warrior song / by Joseph Bruchac — Riffs / by Ann Manheimer — What a song can do / by David Levithan — Piano obsession / by Ibtisam S. Barakat — The audition / by J. Alison James — Tangled notes in watermelon / by Dian Curtis Regan — Ballad of a prodigy / by Jude Mandell — The song of Stones River / by Jennifer Armstrong — The Gypsy's violin / by Gail Giles — New town / by Alexandra Siy — A third kind of funny / by Sarah Ellis.
ISBN 0-375-82499-5 (trade) — ISBN 0-375-92499-X (lib. bdg.)
1. Music—Juvenile fiction. 2. Short stories. [1. Music—Fiction. 2. Short stories.] I. Armstrong, Jennifer, 1961–
PZ5.W4955 2004
[Fic]—dc22 2003024306

Printed in the United States of America
June 2004
10 9 8 7 6 5 4 3 2 1
First Edition

What a Song Can Do

12 riffs on the power of music

edited by

Jennifer Armstrong

Alfred A. Knopf New York

contents

PRELUDE—OVERTURE—INTRO

Music is our first art. When we are babies, our parents hum lullabies to us and sing eensy-weensy spiders up our arms. When we learn our ABCs, we sing them. When our birthday cakes arrive, they come with a fanfare of song and fire. When we make our first excursions into nature, we halt in our tracks to hear the birds sing. We tap our fingers and jiggle our knees up and down as we wait: we are hummers, whistlers, and drummers, passing melodies and rhythms back and forth between our friends like colds. We are musical instruments, and we use instruments of wood and metal and plastic and electricity to fill our world with sound. We just can't help it.

All of us have music in our lives—some of us perform and get paid for it, some of us use music for worship and prayer, some of us sing in the shower, some of us rely upon it for company in the darkness. It's in our elevators and supermarkets, on the car stereo and our cell phones. We carry it with us into every ritual of our lives—our holidays, weddings, and funerals; our inaugurations and graduations; our parades and ballparks; our wars and our peace. There is a musical score to our lives. Where we go, music goes, too.

The stories in this collection offer music in many different keys. There is the companionship of making music with others, of being part of a band, as in Ron Koertge's "Variations on a Theme"; there is the solace of music to the frightened and alone, as in Ibtisam Barakat's "Piano Obsession." J. Alison James's story, "The Audition," gives us the special joy that comes from those frustrating hours of practice that finally pay off in something so much more than the mechanics of violin bow across violin strings.

Music can communicate subtleties that words cannot express—the solid foundation of a boy's identity in Joseph Bruchac's "A Warrior Song," or the sudden opening of a window onto the wide, wide world in Sarah Ellis's "A Third Kind of Funny." Music can be a bridge, and it can be a weapon. It can inspire our imaginations to wonders that cannot be described with pictures or with words, wonders that can only be described by tone, pitch, and harmony. If there is any theme common to these stories, it is that music comforts and supports us in ways too complex and varied to describe with only twelve stories, or perhaps too complex to describe with stories at all—although as writers we keep trying to get closer and closer to the truth, to make music with words. Music is like the air: invisible and indispensable.

This collection is my own house mix. Sample a few cuts or listen all the way through. The stories will show you a little bit of what a song can do.

—Jennifer Armstrong

Ron Koertge
VARIATIONS ON A THEME

Percussion

Mom wanted me to be in the band. You should have heard her quoting the *Reader's Digest*: "Josh," she said, "'practicing and performing with a group builds teamwork and stimulates the brain.'" If that wasn't enough, somebody told her SAT scores tend to be higher among musicians. I think she pictured me playing the snare at Christmas: *tah-rum ta-tum-tum. Isn't that cute.*

Okay, Mom. Fine. Whatever.

I thought I'd hate it, but I loved it. I love percussion. I love drums and drumming. This is just a high school band, okay? For a concert, all I've got to work with are bass, bells, snare, triangle, and cymbals. When we march, it's pretty much *boom, boom, boom* up and down the field. I'm the heart of the band, beating steadily.

But I want to be a drummer after high school. A real drummer like Tris Imboden (Chicago) or Jack Irons (Pearl Jam before Matt Cameron). I want to be in a group, hang with musicians, travel with them, do session work. Eat, breathe, and sleep music. Carry my pad and sticks everywhere. Talk to guys, learn from them, go to concerts, sneak backstage after.

I don't care about sex and drugs. All I want is rock and roll. A lot of guys I know get on the Net and look for pictures of naked girls. I cruise rack toms and floor toms. I scrutinize crash cymbals and drum thrones.

A classic to some people is like Henry Miller's *Tropic of Capricorn*. A classic to me is Jim Chapin's *Advanced Techniques for the Modern Drummer*.

In gym, somebody tells a story about how many girls some quarterback slept with. I tell about the time Mickey Hart (Grateful Dead) got a drum in Tibet made from human skulls and ended up, like, haunted.

The cool thing is, even at this level I run into a lot of maniacs like me. Totally obsessed percussion madmen. One of them sent me this great quote from the philosopher Nietzsche: "Without music, life would be a mistake. I would only believe in a god who knew how to dance."

So maybe God created drummers so there'd always be music He could dance to. And who am I to let God down!

■■■■

I'm not big enough to handle a tuba. I've got braces, so the trumpet is out. And the trombone. And the French horn. My own name is fine (it's Simon). But I like being called by my instrument's name: "Clarinets! Pay attention!"

I'm a follower. Not a sheep, but a team player. There are five of us in the clarinet section. I sit third chair, right in the middle (just like, now that I think of it, I'm the middle child: Rebecca, Mary, Simon, Matthew, John). We're a marching band, we play for assemblies, and we give concerts. I like the uniforms, the way we all look the same. It's cool how personalities dissolve and fifty-two of us turn into a band, the way a million cells turn into a liver or a foot.

What I'm not so crazy about is competition. Being singled out. Whoever sits first chair gets the solos, and it means she's (I'm the only boy clarinet) best. Once a month we audition for Mr. Krieder, the director. I moved up to second chair once, and it made me nervous. Anyway, I advanced by default; the girl ahead of me played really badly.

The next day (and every day after that), I felt her simmering. Since it mattered to her, I didn't practice for the next audition. At all. I tried to sight-read and flubbed everything. I went from second to fourth.

So for a while I sat next to Dorianne Gray. Dorianne cries at every little thing. She's famous for crying. When we go to another school for band contests or workshops, people want to see her cry. She hates being stared at, so she cries. Then they go away.

I was nice to her, just talking and stuff, and pretty soon she liked me. Being liked makes me nervous, too. Relationship-wise, I don't want *pianissimo* (very soft) all the time, but *forte* (loud!) is too much. And I know she expected some kind of crescendo. I could already see it going from "I Want to Hold Your Hand" (Beatles) to "Let's Spend the Night Together" (Rolling Stones) to "She Hates Me" (Puddle of Mudd).

At the next audition, I practiced and moved back to third chair. I couldn't take the pressure.

I'll never be a professional musician. I'm not really gifted like the French horn, who is out of this world. He plays beautifully, if that isn't too gay a thing to say. If I practiced forever, I'd never be better than so-so. And I don't want to end up playing polka tunes or getting gigs at the VFW.

No, when I graduate I'll probably put the old licorice stick away. Lay it out in that case that's red and soft inside like a casket. And close the lid one last time.

Flute

If it wasn't for Josh, I wouldn't be in the band. I joined because he joined; if he quit, I'd quit. I go to rehearsal because he's there. I practice just enough to sit fourth chair.

Guess what the big whoop is in Flute Land: Are

we flutists (rhymes with "cutest"), or are we flautists (rhymes with "stoutest")? Inquiring minds want to know. I can't sleep until I find out! I'm burning up with curiosity!

Yeah, right.

I'm not a stalker or totally obsessed or certifiably nuts, but everything comes down to Josh. Flutes are big on trills, okay? Babbling-brook music. Dancing butterflies. Which always make me think of going on a picnic with Josh. By a stream. Which runs through a meadow. Or it's barefoot-goddess-running-around-with-garlands music. And then falling down all flushed in the grass with Josh dressed like a shepherd.

I think he lifts weights because he's got great arms. His muscles aren't all bunched up like some dumb jock's, but long and silky-looking. For rehearsals he wears a T-shirt with the sleeves cut off and a headband. I swear to god, I want to lick the sweat off him.

Here's the tragic part: he's almost eighteen, which is way, way beyond my fifteen, just like some huge, gorgeous planet with fiery rings and lush vegetation is light-years away from some little asteroid all pitted from meteors and stuff.

I have to admit, though, that sometimes when I'm playing with the band, I end up feeling better. It's like all the loneliness and the invisibleness get washed away by the music. We were working on Handel's *Seven Sonatas* the other day and Mr. Krieder said, "Nice work, Renee. Keep it up." I really liked that. It made me feel like I wasn't just dumb old inexperienced fixated-on-Josh me, but I was a way for the music to get played. Like something was playing me so that I could play it. If that makes any sense.

Anyway, it's a good feeling. Probably not as good as being wrapped in Josh's arms, but pretty darn good.

French Horn

I'm gifted. I've always been gifted, so everybody's used to it. I've learned to be modest. Make that *careful.* Where I come from, you can be special if you don't act special. Then it's live and let live. More or less. Most of the time. I'm still treated a little bit like a rare animal: whispered about, stared at, poked with a stick every now and then to see what will happen.

Our little town is just big enough for privacy, just small enough so nobody's got any real secrets. High school's got a handful of stoners, a few anarchists. They're not bad guys, and after graduation they're going to be working for the Chevrolet dealership out on the belt line or driving a truck for the city. Some of the party girls will get pregnant, then start waitressing out at The Embers, taking their teachers' orders for drinks and steaks. One or two of the FFA kids will go on to the university and major in ag econ. Most will just take over the family farm.

I play French horn and sit first chair. The kids

who sit second and third play music. I'm a musician. I'm already being recruited. When people from places like the Brooklyn Conservatory show up, it's like they bring rarefied air with them. I love talking to those guys. They speak a language I understand, one I'm fluent in (even though I've rarely spoken it before).

My parents don't know what to make of this. Of me. They shrug. "Anthony, it's up to you, son. You know what's best." It's as if two zebras produced an eland. *Who is this strange creature?*

I practice in my room while they watch TV: "Fugue for French Horn and *Seinfeld* Reruns."

I love my instrument. It began as a hunting horn, and in the sixteen hundreds there were beautiful French phrases for the different kinds: the *cor à plusieurs tours* (horn of several turns) or *le huchet* (the horn with which one calls from afar).

It's a beautiful instrument with rich, sonorous tones. The perfect balance of embouchure and air is called "singing on the wind."

That's what I try for every time I perform, while I'm waiting for the wind that will come and carry me away.

Oboe

Funny name, isn't it? French, probably. Mr. Krieder told me, I bet, and I forgot. I forget a lot of stuff. I'm ADD: resource room, homework lab, extra time on tests, earplugs, quiet room = the whole nine yards.

You wouldn't think band would be a good elective for me. Or you'd guess that I'd be the percussion guy: *bomb bomba loo-bomb, a lam-bam-boom!* But no—I'm third-chair oboe. Third of three.

I only joined because a buddy of mine in auto shop plays trombone. He said the kids in band were nice. Easygoing. Bottom line? He said it was fun. I said I'd think about it. My name is Arty, but I'm not arty. If you get my drift.

So I took a look. Just that. One look in the band room. I liked it right away. Liked the way it was organized (like I'm not, I guess). Liked the risers and the tiers of chairs. Liked the music stands, how patient they looked. So I found the director, who's this cool enough guy, and just more or less presented myself. Sort of, Here I am. Now what?

He said he needed an oboe. I liked his no-nonsense approach. Reminded me of somebody who goes into Pep Boys and asks for a rebuilt carburetor.

He walked me over to this locked cabinet, and that was cool, too: valuable stuff inside. Out came this little case with a velvet lining, like the jewel cases rich guys are always giving their tall girlfriends. I watched him put the oboe together and I knew I could do that myself next time, no sweat. I'm good with my hands.

When he soaked the reed, I knew I wanted to play oboe! Details are good for a hyper guy like me. They help me concentrate. While the reed was soaking, Mr. K and I chatted. Can I practice four or five days a week, at least half an hour a day? No problem.

Then he has me just blow on the reed. All by itself. "Pretend," he says, "you're an old geezer with no teeth."

Piece of cake. I make this siren sound and Mr. K grins. When we put the reed in the oboe and he gets my fingers in the right place, I blow again and make—I mean it—a really pretty sound. Mellow. Antique kind of. Reedy in a good way. Like in lush wetlands.

That was two years ago, when I was in ninth grade. Right toward the end of school. So all summer I rode my bike up and practiced.

My friend from shop was right. The other kids are nice. Got some pointers, learned some names, tried out in the fall and made the cut.

Now I've got a girlfriend (plays tuba: lips to die for!), met a lot of people to say hi to. I like the band trips, the bake sales for new uniforms. I like the whole scene.

Twelfth grade next year. Then I graduate. Put my oboe (their oboe, I guess, because I never really owned it) away for the last time.

I don't like to think about that.

Tuba

Okay, I admit it's a weird instrument for a girl, but I'm totally comfortable in my tuba. And I do mean *in* it. I like slipping inside. I like how it curls around me. I've got this fantasy: John Philip Sousa comes over. We chat, hum some stuff together; he leads me on. So I tell him to make himself comfortable, then excuse myself. Two minutes later, I come out of the bedroom wearing nothing but tuba!

A couple of years ago, Mr. Krieder stopped me in the hall and asked if I'd try out. I'd been doing javelin and shot put, but I had a bad elbow. I was looking for something to do.

It was pretty much love at first sight. My lips felt right at home on that big mouthpiece (like they feel right at home on Arty's). And I got the knack of it (that basic *oom-pah-pah*) in no time flat.

I'm not the heart of the band, but I'm essential. And I'm used to that. At home, everybody's younger than me. Mom and I get the other kids off to school while Dad's plowing (we farm about six hundred acres). Mom always says she doesn't know what she'd do without me. Maybe she won't have to. I like to farm, and Dad needs help. I'm big for a girl.

The kids in bands are okay, especially the tubists. Especially at clinics and band camp. We trade tuba jokes: Q: What's the range of a tuba? A: About forty feet, if you're really mad. Q: Hey, did you hear my last solo? A: I sure hope so.

Band camp is famous for sex and drugs, but I don't do drugs, and Arty and I don't do sex. But last year four of us tubists met in one of the camp's big practice rooms, and we played.

God, it was beautiful, and—here's a word right out of English class—plaintive. The room was just full of yearning.

When we were done, we just looked at each other and grinned.

Alto Sax

Charlie Parker, dead at thirty-four (drugs). Lester Young, dead at forty-nine (alcohol). Cannonball Adderley, dead at forty-six (stroke). Paul Desmond, dead at fifty-two (lung cancer). Grover Washington, Jr., dead at fifty-six (heart attack). Roland Kirk, dead at forty-one (stroke).

Not me, man. I'm vegetarian, nonsmoker, clean and sober. I want to go to a college, get a degree, come back and teach in high school. This one. My alma mater. I'm a Booster. I want to lay down the chalk lines for girls' softball, I want to man the grill on the hottest day of the year at the annual street fair. I'll take Neighborhood Watch seriously. Every Saturday night I'll play "Tequila" at the VFW, then "Proud Mary," and finish up with "Good Night, Ladies."

I don't understand that crowd in the back of the bus on the way home from camp or clinics. I know they're only making out, but it's still promiscuity, if you ask me. I've had the same girlfriend since eighth grade. She's a nice girl, a good girl. We've already picked out names for our kids: Samuel and Joshua, Leslie and Amber.

My plan is to retire from teaching at fifty-five or so, work in my garden and play with my grandkids. I don't want to miss out on one minute of my allotted threescore and ten. Not every sax player is a wild man. For every one of those, there's a hundred like me who show up on time and get the job done.

Maybe we don't electrify the crowd and get our names on the marquee, but we always finish the tune, take a bow, pick up the check, and head straight to the bank, where it'll earn two point four percent interest.

Trumpet

My mother wanted me to take piano lessons. She's a good mom but corny beyond belief. Check this out—me with freckles, bent over a Steinway, baseball glove beside me, dog waiting anxiously at my feet, a few pals outside the window yelling for me to come play ball!

Where does she get that stuff, the Nostalgia Channel? I don't have freckles. I never had a dog. My friends have always been hackers and brainiacs, not outfielders.

Dad's the one who turned me on to the trumpet. My ax, as he likes to call it, because he's a big-band freak. Stan Kenton especially. He's still prowling swap meets looking for the McGregor *Stan Kenton and His Orchestra.* His fantasy is me with, say, Lyle Lovett and His Big Band.

It's not gonna happen, but it doesn't hurt to let him dream. I play all right, sit second chair when I practice. But after high school, that's over. Three other guys and I are working on a way to beat Las Vegas. Counting cards at blackjack: hardware implants, computers in our hats. Three geeks bankrolling one high roller. It can be done.

In the meantime, there's the band trips. Not the destination, not the competition. The trip. On the bus. Coming home, especially.

The Greyhound is a country all its own. The front is like the provinces, the outskirts of town, the sticks. (The oboes are up there doing their math homework, okay?) But the back of the bus is like Paris or San Francisco. Somebody's got a hash brownie or two. A pint of vodka.

It's dark. We've just crossed from Somewhere to Elsewhere. We're cruising. People are nuzzling around. Then somebody gets up and changes seats. The kissing continues, just with fresh lips. Nobody's going together, nobody's jealous. We're just kissing in bursts of inspiration and trepidation, like sight-reading a new piece of music.

Love is not an issue. In fact, love is out the bus window someplace, in one of those barely lit barns, probably, where the farmer rubs his horse's ears affectionately even as he slips the bridle on and leads him toward the heavy, shiny plow.

Trombone

I don't know what I'd do without the band. There's it and taking care of my mom. That's my life. And "taking care of my mom" makes it sound like she's sick. She's not. My dad is the sick one. He's a mean drunk, and he won't stop drinking. We've got a lawyer, restraining orders, and everything else we can do legally.

Maybe Mom is sick, too. A little, anyway. She still talks to him on the phone. It's not a pretty sight. She does all this girly stuff like take the phone in the closet and close the door. Or cuddle up in the big chair with the knights-in-armor print and whisper. To him. When he's hungover and all sorry for (1) calling in the middle of the night, (2) driving by and blowing his horn at all hours, (3) throwing beer cans at the door, (4) ambushing her outside of work and yelling at her.

He's forty-two years old. I'm seventeen. Who's the kid here?

Mr. Krieder made sure I talked to the school counselor, who got me a therapist, a guy who drives over from the city once a week and puts in some hours on his way to a degree in Family Counseling. I'm the only one who goes, of course. I'm a one-man family.

Enrique—that's my shrink's name—is helping me see how hard it is for people to change. Dad's not going to. Mom's probably not. And if I don't go away to college next year, all I'll do is guard the entrance to the castle forever. "Is that what you want to do with the rest of your life, Sean?" he asks. "Defend the fair maiden?"

He talks like that because he's into archetypes, but I know what he means.

He makes sure I stay in the band, too. So I've got something of my own. Something non-Mom.

I play the trombone. I alternate between first and second chair, depending on how much practice

I can squeeze in, which depends on how nuts Dad is in any given week.

I usually practice at school. There are maybe twelve little soundproof rooms, and I sign up for one every chance I get. I'd like to get a place of my own someday and be self-contained, you know? No frills. White walls, lean furniture, clean surfaces.

I tell Enrique about wanting to live alone, and he says wait and see. Okay, but I've kind of made up my mind.

Maybe I'm too scarred up to get married, but I'll always have friends. If they're anywhere near as good as the ones I've got now, I'll be fine. Like about a month ago, Dad was on a real bender. So for a few nights some of the guys in the band took turns watching the house. If Dad tried anything, they'd come pouring out of their cars.

Anthony, the French horn genius, took a turn. Here's a guy who gets a split lip or a broken finger and maybe his whole career is shot. He showed up anyway. Because we're friends.

Sometimes at practice, the brass will get a twelve-bar rest and I look around. We're all different, but we put that to one side when we open the sheet music and take that first deep breath.

For as long as the piece lasts, we're not fifty-two personalities scratching and clawing for attention. We're one thing.

We're a band.

Joseph Bruchac

A WARRIOR SONG

The wise Indian elder and the eager youth who hung on his every word stood together beside the beautiful wilderness pond. The sun was just setting over the majestic purple mountains. The sound of two loons, calling to each other in haunting tones, drifted across the bright, still waters.

"Listen close," the old man said. "I am going to teach you a song that the famous Indian athlete Jim Thorpe taught me, back when I was working in Hollywood. It is a warrior song, a song to give you courage. I will sing it to you now and you will always remember it."

Great, I thought, *just when I thought things couldn't get any worse.*

I should probably have begun this story another way, but I couldn't resist trying a little purple prose. When you aspire to be a writer someday, even though you are just a half-breed teenage kid from a hick town in the Adirondacks, you tend to try anything to get attention. Although I suppose I should probably locate the true source of my tendency toward attention-getting where it really belongs. *Meine Mutter.* Much as I love her, my mom has spent at least the last decade of her life trying to figure out ways to make her *junger Liebchen* a big success and, to my horror, some of it has rubbed off on me. Don't blame her for that. She's German. Anyhow, here is another stab at the start of this tale, couched in the language of the AA meetings that my father should have gone to more often.

My name is Mitchell. (Hello, Mitchell.) I'm an Indian, but I can't carry a tune. There's lots of clichés about Indians. For example, there's that whole vanishing race, noble savage thing. Survive instinctively in the forest. Ride a horse as if glued to its back. Speak with animals while having powerful spiritual visions. Cool, no problem. But then there's the music thing. Indians are supposed to be musical. Always singing. And I'm not. Not like Uncle Tommy.

Uncle Tommy Fox, who is of course the wise old Indian elder introduced so dramatically (I hope) at the start of this tale, isn't really my uncle. He's more like a family friend. When I was a little kid, he moved to our small town of Long Pond, way up here in the Adirondacks. He came here to work as a professional Indian in Wild West Town, which is our major summer and fall tourist attraction. Before that, he had been squeaking out a living making jewelry and selling it in the Port Authority down in New York City, so I guess the idea of a job with a regular salary for at least half the year appealed to him.

Uncle Tommy's work description was pretty much the same as my father's. Dress up in buckskin and feathers. Run the archery range ("Three Arrows for a Buck"). Feed the bears and clean out their cages. Do three "Indian Culture" shows a day for the flatlanders (sing, dance, play the flute, and tell wise, lovable, whimsical stories to the snotty-nosed kids who spend much of their time sighting at you down the barrels of their imitation Colt .45s). And, of course, thrice daily, slink into the woods, slap on war paint, hop onto a horse, and join four or five local white guys (who doubled as either cavalry or Indians, depending on which show they were in) to stage fake attacks on stagecoaches and covered wagons filled with happily screaming passengers. Falling backward off his horse when shot by a cap-gun-waving eight-year-old was Uncle Tommy's specialty. My dad preferred just clutching his chest and slumping over his saddle, not having been trained as a stuntman in Hollywood like Uncle Tommy.

Just as soon as he started to work there, Uncle Tommy became real close with my dad. It didn't matter that Uncle Tommy was a whole lot older or that they were from different tribes that used to fight each other—my dad being Abenaki and Uncle Tommy being a Swenoga. The two of them were the only two real Indians in Wild West Town. Back in the days before Uncle Tommy went on the wagon, they spent just about every summer evening after work together. I remember those nights when they would come home singing. I'd be sitting on the back porch waiting, listening to the beeping call of a nighthawk circling the light on the power pole on the corner, or maybe hearing the far-off howl of a coyote from up on the ridge above the town. Eventually I would start to hear Dad and Uncle Tommy, their voices faint as a memory at first, then getting louder and louder. Finally I would see them appear in the circle of light below the power pole, like two actors playing wounded soldiers helping each other across a stage battlefield.

They didn't sing really loud. No matter how drunk they were, they had learned to keep those Indian songs down enough so that none of the neighbors would call the State Police again. But they always sang. Sometimes it would be one of those Lakota sweat lodge songs about Tunkashila, Grandfather Rock. Songs like that are sacred, only supposed to be sung in the sweat lodge, but when they were drunk enough, they probably thought that was where they were. Other times it would be the old Carlisle Indian School fight song that used to be chanted by the whole student body at football games back about a century ago, when Indian teams used to beat the crap out of Michigan and Yale.

Minnewa ka,
Minnewa ka
Minnewa kah wah we . . .

Their long hair would be hanging down over their faces, and at least one of them would be bleeding from whatever bar fight they'd gotten into. My dad, who was a happy drunk (even though they did get into those fights, somehow they always ended up friends with whoever they duked it out with), would be saying to my mom, "You think us Indians look beat up, you ought to see the cowboys." Mom would just nod and help them up the steps. I was big enough, so I would help, too. She'd put Uncle Tommy to bed on the roll-out and get Dad into the bathroom. She was very unemotional and businesslike about it, especially when I was there next to her, helping her put the blankets over my father, wiping his face with a warm washcloth. She only cried later, when she thought I couldn't hear her.

Uncle Tommy got sober before my dad did. He came to our house and apologized to all of us. "I been an old fool," he said. We were all crying and holding hands with each other by the time he was done. We thanked him, even my dad, who said he was going to try to follow Uncle Tommy's example. Nobody sang that night. I didn't hear another Indian song until a week later when my dad came home alone, drunk and singing and complaining how Uncle Tommy wasn't any fun anymore as Mom and I struggled to get his clothes off and get him into bed.

Uncle Tommy began coming over to have dinner with us, usually bringing along some food with him when he came. "I got some good stuff," he would say.

And it was good. Venison, trout he'd caught, wild plants like cattails and fiddlehead ferns. Sometimes he would even cook it for us all. Uncle Tommy's wife had died about ten years before he moved up to Long Pond, so he was pretty expert at cooking. Those dinners were great, especially when Dad had only one or two beers. Uncle Tommy never said a word to Dad about his drinking, but he would bring along this cedar flute he'd made himself, and after dinner he would start playing it. As soon as Uncle Tommy's flute started playing, my father would put down his beer bottle, even if it was still half full. He would sit down in front of Uncle Tommy and just listen to that flute. (And my mom would quietly slip over to pick up Dad's beer bottle and pour the rest of it out into the sink.) I don't know what my father heard in those flute songs Uncle Tommy played. I know that I could close my eyes when I was listening and it was as if I was all alone with that flute, somewhere so deep in the woods that no road had ever reached there.

Finally, one of those nights after Uncle Tommy had finished playing his flute, my father cleared his throat.

"I guess I am ready to go to a Meeting," he said.

Dad was in his second year of going to Meetings when the accident happened. He hadn't been drinking, but there were empty beer bottles in the cab of the truck that swerved across the center line and crashed into his car. Uncle Tommy played "Amazing Grace" and the "Zuni Sunrise Song" on his flute at Dad's funeral.

I don't know why I've told you all of this. But Mr. Wilson, who is my Creative Writing teacher at Long Pond High, says that when you write a story you should put everything you think you know into it. That way you can find out what the real mystery is. Plus you can go back later and cut out all the stuff that doesn't really fit. Which is probably most of what I just told you. Like what does Uncle Tommy and my dad singing old Indian songs have to do with my having a tin ear? Or with the fact that my mom is so eager for me to get more into music now that it is my junior year and seeing as how I vill soon be trying to get into the colleges, *ja,* and we bot' know dat der colleges vant students who are vell-rounded. *Ja.*

You'd think she would have given up by now. This whole music thing has been going on between me and her ever since she gave me my first rattle and I used it like a crowbar to break out of my crib. *Ja,* sure, I loved the lullabies she sang to me, and they are as stuck in my head as ten-day-old chewing gum is to the bottom of a sneaker. And they weren't just German lullabies, either. Blond, blue-eyed, and Teutonic as she is, my mom has always been crazy for anything Indian. (Thus my father, as well as her illogical tolerance for her only son's many failings.) She learned at least twenty different Indian lullabies—only one of which my father had ever heard of, even remotely. She sang so many of them to me every night that I was eventually stunned into slumber. Plus she put this tape player in my room and kept it going—at just a low enough volume to drive me nuts—with recordings of Pueblo Turtle Dance songs, Iroquois Round Dances, Creek Stomp Dances, Kiowa Buffalo Songs, et maddening cetera. She bought every darn tape in the Canyon Records catalog. That was why I used that rattle like a crowbar to pry open the slats of my crib. I just had to get to that music-making torture box and make it stop.

When she thought I was old enough, Mom took me to my first music lessons. Piano. Three months later, the teacher had a little conference with my mother.

"Mitchell," she said, a bright, slightly hysterical smile pasted onto her face, "is a very determined young man." Then she stated her firm opinion that until piano benches came equipped with seat belts to keep me from hopping off and heading for the hills whenever her back was turned, we were wasting our time.

Over the years, we made our way through every full- and semi-professional instructor of music within a radius of fifty miles. Cello (I kept getting the bow wedged between the strings), clarinet (I ate the reeds), even banjo (having been reduced to bluegrass after the grapevine of classical music teachers got the word out so thoroughly about Mitch the Terrible that any phone call from a woman with a German accent seeking lessons for her son would be answered with either a quick disconnect or a polite "You have the wrong number, ma'am") was a failure. So for a time, my mom backed off. It was enough that I was good in sports and had decent grades.

However, there is this thing that starts happening to some parents when their kids hit that age when the possibility of college looms above them like a big rock about to roll down and obliterate everything in its path. It is the "I must do everyting dat I can to get my vonderful child into der best college" syndrome. So once again, the idea of making Mitch musical, of drawing out whatever hidden symphonies must surely be buried deep within, was occupying my mother's mind. She was going to bring out the music in me or die trying. But instead of going at it in the usual way, instead of trying that old failed route of sending me off to a new round of teachers who had, perhaps, never gotten the word about the legendary Indian kid who had actually managed to step on a banjo while he was being taught how to play it, this time she attacked me at my weakest point. She used Uncle Tommy.

Even though I might joke some about it, Uncle Tommy really is the most important adult in my life, aside from my mother. He really does know things, and I'm always learning from him. He has this way of teaching that is like aikido—it just turns things around and focuses them right back at you. Attack and you find yourself flat on your back. Go with the flow, like a tree bending in the wind, and you stay rooted and strong. And that was how it was this time. Just when I was in the middle of a start-of-summer-vacation, tune-out-the-rest-of-the-world mood, he showed up at our door in that old pickup truck of his and asked if I could come along and give him a hand with something.

"Sure," I said. I grabbed my work gloves, figuring that we were going to be taking down the old toolshed. That toolshed has been trying to fall down in Uncle Tommy's backyard for as long as I can remember. All it would take to knock it down, it has seemed for years, would be a good strong wind. But the beams inside it are old ones, made of oak, and it is stronger than it looks.

"Lotta good wood in there," Uncle Tommy had said to me. "Nex' summer you hep me take it down, eh, Mitchell?"

But once I got into the truck, Uncle Tommy spun the wheel so that we did a U-turn, right in front of a loaded log truck on Route 9. Waving his open right hand and smiling sweetly in response to the driver's single-finger salute, Uncle Tommy drove us right down to the far end of the lake, where the oldest cedars leaned over the water.

And so here we were. Me waiting for whatever it was that Uncle Tommy was going to throw at me and him just sitting there like an old turtle nodding on a rock in the sun. And then, which is where you came in, he told me to listen to that song.

Listen. That is Uncle Tommy's favorite word. He says that is where every story in the whole world begins. So even though I groaned inwardly when he told me to listen close, that he was going to teach me a song, I really did listen. Then, as those two loons whooped and yodeled back and forth to each other way out on Long Pond, he sang Jim Thorpe's song.

"Whey hey," he sang. *"Maya tohna ley . . ."*

He didn't tell me what the song meant, just that Big Jim Thorpe had taught it to him. But I didn't need to have the words translated. After all, most of our old songs can't really be translated into English. It isn't, like some anthropologist or somebody said, that we've forgotten our old languages. It is that those songs were never meant to be translated into anything other than that language. Their real language is that ancient one spoken by the drumbeat of the heart.

You know who Jim Thorpe is, don't you? He was an Oklahoma Indian kid of the Sac and Fox Nation. When he won both the decathlon and the pentathlon in the 1912 Olympics, the King of Sweden said that he was the greatest athlete in the world. "Thanks, King," is what Jim said in return. Then, a few years later, when they discovered Jim had played minor league baseball for a couple of summers before the Olympics, they took away his gold medals.

Big Jim Thorpe was my dad's biggest hero. I think Dad identified with him so much not just because he was an athlete, like my dad had been when he was young, and another Indian, but because Big Jim got screwed by the system. Just like my dad "and every other Indian who has ever tried to stand up for himself," as Dad used to say when he was drinking. And that was yet another reason why Dad liked Big Jim, because old Big Jim had more than a passing acquaintance with the bottom of a bottle. For a while, in those years when my dad was drinking so much, I hated Jim Thorpe.

Uncle Tommy, though, loved Jim Thorpe. He didn't love him just because he was Indian or because he was the world's greatest athlete or because he was also a world-class boozer. He loved Jim Thorpe because after he met him, he learned two things about Big Jim. The first was that he had, as Uncle Tommy put it, "one of the most kindest and generousest hearts." He would give you the shirt off his back if he thought you were cold. In fact, Uncle Tommy saw him do just that one cool Southern California night when they were walking together along Hollywood Boulevard. Big Jim saw an old wino lady shivering in an alleyway, and he just peeled off his sweater and wrapped it around the old woman.

The second was that Big Jim was great at singing Indian songs. It was because of Indian songs that Uncle Tommy met Big Jim and got his own chance in pictures. It had been back in those years before World War II when Uncle Tommy was in Hollywood, a star-struck little Indian boy who had hitchhiked all the way out there to become a movie Indian. Looking for work and finding it were two different things, though. It wasn't all that easy to be a Hollywood Indian back in those days unless you were an Italian. Most of the actors playing Indians back then weren't really Indian. Directors liked the way Italians looked when they dressed them up in buckskin and feathers. If you could speak Italian, it was easier for you to get a job playing an Indian.

One day, after he'd been out there for a couple of months, Uncle Tommy was just sitting on a corner near the Hollywood Bowl, playing a song on a cedar flute. People were dropping coins into his cowboy hat, which he had on the ground next to him. Then a big man with a craggy face came up and stood there, watching and listening to his song. When Uncle Tommy was done, that man dropped a whole dollar into his hat.

"Thank you," Uncle Tommy said.

"Che bello!" the man said. *"Ciao, paesan."*

Uncle Tommy looked up at him and shook his head. He didn't understand a word of Italian at the time. He only learned it later when he needed to use it during the filming of stuff like *They Died with Their Boots On,* where Uncle Tommy was one of the Indians who plugs Errol Flynn (playing the part of George Armstrong Custer) with an arrow.

"You a real Indi'n?" the man asked, a big grin spreading across his face.

"Swenoga," Uncle Tommy said.

A right hand that looked as big as a grizzly bear's paw was held out to him. Uncle Tommy took it and the big man hauled Uncle Tommy up to his feet as if he were lighter than a feather.

"Son," he said, "my name's Jim Thorpe. And if you can shoot a bow and arrow as well as you can play that flute, I can get you a job in pictures."

Big Jim was just as good as his word. A day later, Uncle Tommy was standing in line along with all the other actors playing redskins, waiting to be coated with spray paint so that he would look red enough to look like a real movie Indian.

"Hollywood," Uncle Tommy said to me, "taught me how to succeed in the Indian bizniz. It is sure a lot harder, Mitchell, to play a Indian than to be one."

Hearing Uncle Tommy's stories about Jim Thorpe, about his kindness and his love of real Indi'n music, made me stop hating Big Jim. Of course it wasn't really Big Jim that I was hating. I guess you know that. But until this day, sitting here by Long Pond, Uncle Tommy had never actually shared with me one of those songs he said Jim Thorpe sang.

So that made me listen even closer. I just had a feeling I was going to learn something from that song. Sure, I would forget it as soon as I heard it. I knew that as far as music was concerned, I was like

Teflon. No tunes stick to my surface. A funny thing happened, though. As I listened to Uncle Tommy sing that song, it began to sound familiar. In fact, it sounded suspiciously like another song Uncle Tommy had tried to teach me a year ago. An Apache traveling song. And how the hell was I remembering that? Then I began to remember another song. This one was a Choctaw Stomp Dance that Uncle Tommy had tried to teach me the summer I was helping him out at Wild West Town. And now, strangest of all, the song coming back to me was one of those that my dad and Uncle Tommy used to sing when they were coming home drunk. Except this time I wasn't hearing their drunk voices. I was hearing the voices of two good-hearted men singing together, singing strong and clear and sober. Before long, as Uncle Tommy sang and kept on singing, it was like I was in the middle of a cloud of songs. Songs were everywhere, circling around me like birds, flying to me, flying through my heart.

There is something you should know about Indian songs. They may be short, but they are really long. What I mean is that even if they have only a few words, they can still be sung for a *looooong* time. Like if you are singing a song for the corn to come up, that song can go on so long it seems as if the corn should already be five feet tall by the time it is finished. It was that way by the lake. Uncle Tommy just kept singing that song, repeating what seemed like the same verse again and again. It might have been boring to some listeners. On some other day it would have seemed that way for me. But today it didn't. For some reason, the more he sang that song, the more I heard in it. It was like layer upon layer being laid down—each layer lifting you up a little higher. Or maybe it was more like someone digging down into the earth with their hands, digging the soil away gently. And even though every handful of soil might look just the same, every handful helped you go deeper; every handful exposed more of the roots.

Uncle Tommy stopped singing, but the song didn't stop. It went on and on, and it took me a minute to realize that I was the one who was singing it. When I finally stopped, that song echoed out over the lake. Then the loons started up again, and they were calling to the rhythm of that same song. I wiped my eyes and looked over at Uncle Tommy, nodding my head.

Uncle Tommy nodded back. "It is jes' that way, Mitchell," he said, placing his hand on a cedar branch that might one day be a flute. "Sometimes it jes' takes the songs a while to find their way out of you."

There is a smell when someone is sick. It's always the same, no matter where you are, no matter when it is, no matter what the illness. It's sweet. Too sweet. Like a diabetic's urine.

I knew it smelled like that in my parents' bedroom, but it had always smelled like that, so I never noticed it anymore, not even when I dipped the stick into the urine sample Mom handed me and selected the right insulin dose. She used to give herself her own shots, when she could see. Now I chose the amount, fitted the vial onto the hypodermic, and plunged it through her skin, into her thigh.

"Okay, Mom." I threw out the stick and dumped the sample down the toilet.

"Have a good day, Lee."

They'd named me Nathan so they could practice the *th* sound. There is no such sound in Polish, Yiddish, or Hebrew, the languages they knew best from growing up Jewish in Poland, before the Nazis came. Still, they almost always called me by my middle name, Lee.

"See you later." I kissed her cheek and waved goodbye to Dad, who was calling clients from the kitchen phone.

The sun's glare reflected off the old Chevy in our driveway. Mornings can be blinding in L.A., especially after the darkness in my house. I banged my books against the car's rear as if it were a horse's rump. Nothing could get me down today. Not even a dead car.

We'd won last night, me and the Wombats. We placed first in the 1968 Battle of the School Bands, and we were going to play in the all-district concert at the Hollywood Bowl this Friday night. Even Dad was impressed. My brother promised he'd help me start the Chevy so I could drive us all there in style. Or at least in a car.

I made it through the school day, doodling guitars on my papers. When Mr. Kovner asked me to discuss the imagery of dawn in the *Odyssey,* all I could talk about was Hendrix's guitar riff in "Castles Made of Sand." The class cracked up. Mr. Kovner didn't say anything. I thought he must have been pretty angry at me until I caught a glimpse of his grading sheet and saw an A+ next to my name for class participation.

Things were going so well, the blanket of silence at home didn't even bother me that afternoon. There was a note; Mom had gone out with the lady from the Braille Institute. Dad was visiting clients. And Stan . . . well, Stan didn't live there anymore.

I was slathering mayonnaise on a piece of Wonder Bread—being alone isn't quite so lonely with a bologna sandwich in your hand—when the call came.

"Is this Lee?" The female voice was young and breathy, like Marilyn Monroe's. "This is Sheila? I'm a volunteer with the Braille Institute?" She pronounced every sentence as if it were a question, until she reached the point of the phone call. "I'm sorry. I tried calling your father's office, but he's not there."

Of course not. He's with clients.

"It's your mother."

I could see the imprints my fingers made through the mayonnaise into the bread.

"She's at Cedars of Lebanon, under good care. They say she'll be fine in a few days."

I mumbled something polite and hung up as fast as I could. There was no way to reach Dad. I left a message with the receptionist at his office, but he wouldn't call in until he came home. That's the way it is with insurance salesmen. Then I tried Stan—the dial's round return between each number was so slow, I thought I'd go crazy—but he didn't answer, of course. He'd be on campus in the middle of the day.

If only I could get the Chevy started, I could drive to the hospital now and come back for Dad when he got home. Dad had insisted on keeping the Chevy for me, not letting Stan take it when he moved out. But now that I finally had my license, the car refused to go. I washed the dishes from my sandwich plus the ones left over from breakfast, then went outside and opened the hood. I was checking the oil and the belts when Dad came up the walk from the bus stop.

"Norek, what are you doing?" Norek. The nickname Dad used for me when he was in a good mood. That wouldn't last. "You are a mess!" He started brushing off the dirt and grime that clung to my T-shirt. "What about homework? You will be like Stan. You will never get into medical school if . . ."

I waited until we were inside to tell him. I knew how his face would shift; I'd seen it many times—his creases deepened; his lips thinned; his skin flushed then paled.

"What was she doing, that Braille lady? Why did she have your mother march like a soldier all around the city?" he demanded.

"They were at the art museum."

"Art museum. Huh. What good is art to a blind woman."

"She can still see some things. And just getting out of the house . . ."

"What about insulin you give her? Are you certain it is right dose?" His Polish accent always got thicker when he was upset.

"I'm sure. The stick read—"

"Call a taxi." He walked into the living room. "From the hospital, you will call Stanusz."

▪ ▪ ▪ ▪

In a hospital, the smell of medicine disguises the smell of sickness underneath. Lights are too bright, sounds clang and echo, and nurses smile too much.

The signs said "Children Under 16 Are Not Allowed in the Wards." Nobody questioned me, even though I'd turned sixteen only a couple of months ago. But I was used to people thinking I was older when they knew my parents were not my grandparents. Also, I looked older, which would have been great for buying booze, if I'd wanted to.

I stood back as Dad pulled open the curtain surrounding Mom's bed. Her face was gray, the same as the once-white sheets she lay on. An IV tube ran from her arm to an upside-down bottle. I could barely hear her when she said, "Hello, Yosef . . . Lee."

Sheila, the lady from the Braille Institute, was sitting in an orange chair next to the bed. I knew who she was immediately, since she looked the way her voice sounded—dyed blond hair, busty, a starlet type. She stood as soon as we walked in.

"I'm so sorry—I don't know what happened—Everything was fine, then she went suddenly pale and started shaking—I tried to reach you and your sons—Then I drove her to the hospital—I couldn't think of anything else . . ."

"You are a lovely young woman," Dad said, "but

did you not know my wife is diabetic? Why do you traipse her around like she is healthy? Doesn't the Institute tell you about the people you take places?"

Sheila slowly turned red as Dad spoke. After a moment, she fished in her purse for a card and handed it to him. Her voice was no longer breathy. "I am very sorry, Mr. Witkowski. I did my best. If you are unhappy, feel free to call the Institute." Her high heels clicked as she left the room.

"I will!" Dad called after her, then turned to Mom. "We will make them a case."

She blinked at him. "Yosef, don't. It wasn't her fault."

"No? Then why are you in the hospital?"

"Always you do this. You think I like it here? But that Sheila, she did her best. We are not in Poland, and you are not an attorney anymore. Don't make a case. Please."

"After twenty years in this country, I know about American law, Miriam." Dad's voice was low and stern. "Somebody is always at fault."

Then Mom started talking high and fast, in Polish. I wasn't sure she even knew I was there, so I left to look for a phone to call Stan. Instead, I ran into him getting off the elevator.

He greeted me, as always, with a punch to my shoulder. "Hey, kid. How is she?"

"She can't be too bad. They're fighting."

He snorted a laugh, then lit a cigarette.

A short blond nurse chirped, "No smoking in the hallways, sir."

He grinned and winked at her. "Sorry." He tossed the cigarette on the floor and stomped it out. "What'd the doc say?"

"We haven't seen him yet."

"You haven't?" His face clouded. "C'mon." He started to steer me toward the nurse's station when Dad came out of the room.

"Ha! Look who is here!" Dad's tone took on the sarcastic edge he almost always used with Stan.

"Hi, Dad."

"How nice of you to take time from your busy day to visit your sick mother."

"I was in the lab. I didn't know about it until I got home and the Braille Institute called."

"If you would ever call home, maybe you would know sooner."

Stan called home a lot, I thought, but neither of us said anything. He clenched and unclenched his fists, then said quietly, "Okay, Dad."

A young doctor introduced himself and explained that something had gone wrong with the way Mom was reacting to the insulin. "We're trying different kinds of medicine to put everything back in balance."

"Where is Dr. Lanneman?" Dad demanded.

"He will call you as soon as he can."

Dad remained stonily silent during the rest of the young doctor's explanation. On the way back to Mom's room, he grumbled, "Dr. Lanneman had better call tonight, or I will make him remember me . . ."

We talked to Mom for a few minutes. Stan asked her to keep track of the prettiest nurses.

"And how am I to know who is pretty and who is not?" She smiled weakly. She had a different smile when I was younger.

"By their voices, Mom," Stan was saying. "Or better yet"—he leaned over and whispered into her ear, loud enough for me to hear—"by their touch." He winked at me.

"If you chased girls less and worked more," Dad said, "you would have gotten into medical school."

We didn't stay long. Mom was getting tired, and Stan had an early-morning seminar. As we left the building, Dad insisted that we take the bus home; he didn't want to pay for another taxi.

"I'll come by tomorrow and help you start the Chevy," Stan promised. "It's probably just the battery." He kicked up the motorcycle's stand.

Dad sneered. "Everyone thinks you are a hoodlum when you ride this thing."

"When 'everyone' wants to buy me a car," Stan said with a shrug, "I'll be more than happy to accept."

I called Elliott as soon as we got home—band practice was just starting, and Neil could pick me up. I was on my way out the door, guitar in hand.

"Your mother is sick, and you go out?"

"We've got to practice, Dad."

"What kind of selfish son goes out when his mother is in the hospital?"

"The concert's in three days."

"You have no dinner?"

"I'll eat when I get home."

"No homework?"

"I finished it at school."

He shook his head, then said, "When will you be home?"

"Eleven-thirty."

"Be home ten-thirty."

▪▪▪▪

Dad was in Mom's room, sitting in the orange chair, when I got there after school the next day. He'd been at the hospital since morning, using the pay phone to cancel his meetings.

Mom looked worse. Her eyes blinked open.

"Lee." She patted my hand. "How is your band?" At least she asked, even if she didn't wait for the answer. "Where is the button to put the bed up? I want to sit higher, to see you. These nurses, they don't show me a thing."

"They're busy," I said, putting her hand on the control.

"Too busy to help a patient who needs help," she said. "Yosef, when can I go home?"

▪▪▪▪

I took the bus home alone and got back with enough time to study and still practice. I was working on my lead solo for "All Your Love" when I heard the taxi door close. I jumped to put away my guitar, but Dad came in before I could fish the case out from underneath my schoolwork.

"You practice?"

I nodded.

He hung his coat carefully in the hall closet, then sat next to me on the couch and took off his left shoe, then his right. He set them neatly next to each other.

"Lee," he said, "you cannot play Friday night. This I think you already know."

When somebody says the last thing you want to hear—even if you expected it without knowing you expected it—your body gets real sweaty, you start to shake, and your mind lets go of anything you might have said. My brain felt as clumsy and stupid as my hands.

But it wouldn't have done any good, even if I could've thought of something to say. Stan would've thought of something. And he and Dad would've started shouting, and Stan would've punched a wall and gone slamming out of the house, unless Dad did that first. And Mom would've cried, "You selfish son! Why do you cause your father such grief?" And I would've sat in my room, like always.

Which is what I did then. Same result, without the shouting.

There was always something. When I was a kid, it was stuff like Little League and Boy Scouts, things other kids did that I never could because I had to help with the laundry or go to the store or vacuum or do the dishes. Even music. After the Beatles came on the scene and everybody started taking guitar lessons, I couldn't. We couldn't afford it. I didn't like it, but it was okay. I understood why it happened. We were different. From everybody.

We weren't supposed to be alive.

Finally I taught myself on a cheap nylon-string guitar that Stan brought back from Germany when he was in the army. He ended up giving it to me when I ended up being the one who played it. And now I had this great used electric Gibson Melody Maker and a Fender Deluxe amp that I'd bought after spending all summer pumping gas at Manny's. I shoved the Gibson under my bed, out of sight.

Practice time rolled around. Dad had eaten at the hospital and didn't ask if I wanted dinner. There'd be chips or something at Elliott's; his mom always made sure we had stuff to eat. When I heard Neil drive up, I grabbed my guitar and hurried to the door.

"Where are you going?" Dad had the TV up loud, like always—he was hard-of-hearing from when he worked with loud machinery in a clothing factory.

"To band practice!" I shouted to be heard. "I'll be back early!"

"Good. Tell them they must find another guitar player."

▪▪▪▪

Elliott's living room already had that warm electrical smell that happens when instruments have been on for a while. I joined them on "All Your Love," we did a couple of Yardbirds numbers, and then we tried "Castles Made of Sand."

I played better that night than I could ever remember playing. I felt as though I were whirling and soaring with the notes, up into space, away from Elliott's house, from school, from Dad and Mom and all the yelling, away even from Stan. Away from the hospital and anything that smelled of sickness.

There are no smells in space.

No words, either.

Behind me, Neil kept the beat, Elliott did some nice chording, and Melnick pulled off a few cool riffs on his bass. Elliott's vocals sounded good, I think, but I wasn't listening to the words. Just to the beat and the notes that rushed out of my guitar as if it were the last chance they'd have to be heard.

I packed up after a short set. "Gotta go home," I mumbled.

"Aw, man, it's not even ten-thirty yet." Melnick kept his fingers over the bass's strings to silence them.

Neil shoved his flopping blond hair off his forehead. "We got only two days till the concert. You can't split now."

I shrugged into my jacket. "Got to," I said. "Sorry."

"You comin' to practice tomorrow night?" Elliott was peering at me.

"Maybe."

"What's up, man?" Elliott said. "You're the one who's always on us to practice."

"I'm sorry. Mom's back in the hospital, and

Dad . . ." I couldn't finish the sentence, so I shrugged again.

"He doesn't want you playing Friday." Elliott knew my family pretty well.

I shrugged and nodded at the same time.

"What're you gonna do?" Melnick put his bass down.

"There's not much I *can* do."

Elliott ran his fingers through his curly hair—a "Jewfro," he called it. "I dunno. It's like the track team, isn't it?"

Elliott was the captain of the track team because I wasn't on it anymore. I was supposed to be captain this year, but I kept missing meets and finally had to quit when Dad needed me to paint the house.

Melnick was saying something about finding another guitar player.

"How about Mickey?" I suggested. "His band came in second. He's good."

"You're better," Elliott grumbled.

"Thanks. I think."

"Y'know, why don't you just play," he said. "What's your dad gonna do?"

I snorted. Elliott was great, but he didn't understand. Nobody did, except maybe Stan. It's like living with World War II still going on so that, when somebody mentions "the War," you don't think about Vietnam first—you think about Nazis and concentration camps. It's like thinking that every backfire you hear is a gunshot, and every little earthquake is a bomb. It's like keeping too much food around in case you can't get any the next day, or like accepting a hand-me-down fry pan with a broken handle because maybe you can use it sometime, or like never telling anyone you are Jewish. It's knowing everybody hates you. It's never trusting anyone, not even other refugees. Not even your own son.

But he'd saved us. Well, he saved Stan and Mom, anyway. Even though my grandparents and uncles and aunts were all killed by the Nazis, Dad got Stan and Mom out of Poland and into safe hiding—and near starvation—on a farm in southern France. Me, I was born later, after they got to America. After the War.

But in West Los Angeles in the 1960s, the War was very much still going on.

How do you disobey the man who saved your family from the Nazis?

▪▪▪▪

Stan was leaning over the Chevy's engine when I got home from school the next day.

"Look, here and here." He used the wrench to point out the bolts that held down the battery. "And the cables, here and here." The veins in his biceps bulged as he attacked one of the bolts. "We'll take it to Manny's and trade it in."

"Okay." I wiped off some of the leaves and berries that littered the car.

"You do the next one."

He handed me the wrench. I leaned over,

breathing in the thick smell of oil and gas, smells that always made me think of my brother. I fitted on the wrench and pulled, then pulled harder. Stan handed me the 3-IN-ONE, but it didn't help. The bolt wouldn't budge. Maybe if I had veins that bulged, I thought, I could get it off. Finally Stan took over, and after a lot of cursing in Polish (he never swore in English around me), he handed me the bolt. We tied the battery to the bookrack on the back of his Honda. He insisted we wear helmets even for the short ride to Manny's, where we picked up some 30-weight oil and a cheap used battery.

"It'll do ya," Manny told us, "and you can use the money you saved by not buying a new one to get yourselves haircuts."

After Stan installed the "new" battery in the Chevy, I set the oilcan pouring through the funnel and put hose water into the radiator. It took a few tries—we had to take off the air filter and fiddle with the carburetor—but finally the car started and hummed like a dream.

"Get in," Stan said.

I went for the passenger door.

"Not there." He nodded to the driver's side.

"All right!" I didn't care if I sounded too eager. Not around my brother.

Inside, the Chevy smelled heavily of mildew. The springs squeaked a little when I sat down. I ran my hands over the cold steering wheel. It seemed very big.

"Put her in reverse, Nate." Stan rolled down his window and flicked out his cigarette ashes.

I let the car roll slowly backward out of the driveway, pumping the brakes a little to be sure they still worked. I came to a full stop on the street, wrestled the automatic shift lever into drive, then rolled down my window and rested my arm on the doorframe.

Stan blew out a puff of smoke. "Two hands on the wheel, kid."

I drove the neighborhood streets slowly at first, turning where Stan told me to turn, stopping where he told me to stop. It felt as if I were learning to drive all over again, and I sort of was. It had been a couple of months since I'd passed the test.

I thought we could talk about the concert while we were driving, but at first Stan was so busy telling me what to do, there wasn't a chance. When we both got used to me behind the wheel, the quiet was so comfortable, I didn't even want to turn on the radio. I just wanted to feel the rumble of the motor, the rush of wind through the vents and windows, and my brother's silent presence next to me. It wasn't until I swung the car back into the driveway and set the parking brake that he asked, "So how are you and Dad doing?"

I shrugged.

"Yeah? He sounded pretty eager for me to get the car started. I guess you'll be driving him back and forth to the hospital as long as Mom's there."

"That's why he wants it."

"And you want it for tomorrow night."

I didn't say anything.

"Yeah." Stan went into the house and came out a few minutes later with a cup of coffee. I sat next to him on the front step. "So what is it you're not telling me, kid?"

I stared across the street, as if a beautiful girl were passing by. "He won't let me play in the concert."

Stan took a gulp of coffee and set the cup on the warm cement. "You surprised?"

"In a way, yes. In a way, no."

"What are you going to do?"

"What can I do?"

"You can play."

"Right."

"Don't be so cocky. I mean it. You've got your driver's license. And now you've got a car. Drive him to the hospital and meet the rest of your band at the Bowl."

"How can you say that? You know what he does when you don't do things his way."

"Oh, yeah." A grin twisted across Stan's face. "He insults you. Then he stops talking to you. Then he doesn't let you use 'his' stuff—like the cameras or the cars he can't use anyway. Then he insults you more. Then he tells you to do all the chores he's let pile up—the shopping, the cleaning—and if you don't do them, you feel like you're turning him over to the Nazis."

"Remember how he used to tell me he would call the police if I misbehaved?"

"And you always believed him." Stan snorted, then added, "Sometimes I think you still do."

I tossed a pebble into the bushes. "So how can you say I can play?"

"Because I know what it does to you when you only do things his way."

I let the crackle of his cigarette package and the strike of the match take up the silence. I put my open hand out.

"Can I have one?"

"Uh-uh," he said. "I'm not letting you get addicted to this shit."

The phone rang. It was Elliott. He wanted to know what was happening.

"I'm still working on it," I told him.

"Mickey's gonna be at practice tonight."

"Oh." Why did it feel so bad that they'd taken my advice?

▪▪▪▪

I stowed my guitar in the trunk of the Chevy before Dad got home. Not that it mattered. He'd understand that I had to go to practice to show Mickey what I do. I figured it would just be better if he didn't see it.

Even though the evening was cool, I rolled down the car window while we drove to the hospital so I could rest my elbow on the doorframe and steer with one hand. Dad watched without saying anything. He clung to the armrest the whole way.

I went in with him and stayed for a short while. Dad didn't argue about my leaving, since I was doing what I had to do to get out of playing the next night. Mom didn't say much. She usually didn't when she was in the hospital. She hated being there.

The guys were already working on "All Your Love" when I showed up. Mickey had the tongue-sticking-out-of-your-mouth stare they show in all the guitar magazines, and his jeans had holes in all the right places. I listened for a few minutes. He played fast, the notes flying from his fret board. People who don't know better are impressed with that even when it gets sloppy, the tones mushing into each other. Not many would notice how his riffs wandered sometimes into other keys and went higher when Melnick was playing lower, so it felt like the band was splitting when it should have been most together.

Nobody else would notice, I told myself.

"Hey, man, sorry to hear you can't play." Mickey shook my hand.

"Yeah. Listen, at that turnaround . . ."

He nodded as I told him how he should go down, with Melnick. They went over it again. He went up again. We went over it one more time; he did it again.

"Y'know, I got my own way of doing things," he said.

That was true. I was trying to make the band sound the way it sounded with me playing, and it couldn't, not without me. Mickey and I both joined in on the next number. At first, trading riffs with him was fine, but then he held on, playing so fast that when my turn came, he didn't stop; he just kept going, up and down the fret board. They finished the song with me doing rhythm along with Elliott, who threw me a look, and I knew he was thinking what I was, that Mickey liked flash too much.

I fished out my guitar case from under the pile of jackets. "Guess there's not much I can do here." The closing clasps sounded like gunshots.

"Sorry, man," Mickey said. "I just got goin' there, y'know?"

Elliott walked out to the car with me. "So what's gonna happen tomorrow?"

"I don't know." I put the guitar in the trunk and slammed it closed.

"That's not good enough."

"What do you want me to do? My mom's in the hospital. You want me to abandon her and my dad?"

"No. I want you to play." There was a pause; then he continued. "You know Mickey's not good enough. On 'All Your Love,' maybe, but we'd be a joke up there on anything else."

"I know."

"We need you, Nate."

Elliott turned and walked into his house without looking back.

I kept the radio off the whole way to the hospital, where Dad was waiting to be picked up. The music on the car's AM was lousy anyway, and it just seemed I could drive better without the noise of the announcer and the commercials. It seemed I could smell the engine better, too, and see the stars, and hear the motor. Everything seemed clearer without the blaring of words.

"The doctor says she is doing better. But where do they get their nurses?" Dad said when he got in the car. "They don't check on her. They don't give her sleeping pills or insulin shots on time. She will die in the hospital with that kind of care. If anything happens, I will make them a case."

"I know, Dad." I steered the car out of the lot, keeping the window rolled up.

"She does better, I think. Dr. Lanneman says she will come home tomorrow. It is good you are not playing the concert."

I had to slam on the brakes at a red light I almost didn't see.

"You will drive better than this when you take her home tomorrow."

If they took a taxi, I thought, he wouldn't have to worry about my driving.

As if he'd been reading my mind, Dad said, "You will drive. Your mother will not return from the hospital in a taxi. She will come home in our own car."

All I wanted to do when we got home was sleep, but Dad had different ideas. He started collecting the laundry and wiping the kitchen counters. "You vacuum. Your mother will not come home to a dirty house."

Why not? I thought. She usually lived in one. I pulled out the vacuum. Maybe Stan got his muscles from lugging around that heavy machine, I thought hopefully as I watched the nozzle suck up dirt, pulling and fluffing the squashed-down pile of the rug. The place looked pretty good when I got done.

Dad'll be happy, I thought. Mom won't notice. Elliott will be pissed that I won't make it after all. And me?

I dragged the vacuum back into the closet and shut the door tightly.

▪▪▪▪

Nobody at school the next day would talk about anything but the band concert. Elliott and the guys kept pretty much together, with Mickey hanging around with them, too. Which wasn't unusual—we were friends. Maybe I just noticed it more because I wasn't hanging out with them. I couldn't.

I gave Elliott a lift home after school.

"The moment of decision approaches," he said.

"Mom's getting out today. I don't think I can make the concert. I've got to drive her home."

"Your dad's taken taxis as long as I've known you, and all of a sudden he can't?"

"Looks that way."

"What time you gonna spring her?"

"I don't know. Dad's there now. I'm heading over after I drop you off."

"I got the band order. We're not on till the second half; that means around nine-thirty. You can get her and still be there."

I thought how it would be, picking up Mom, taking her home, then leaving.

"Think about it," Elliott said as I pulled into his driveway.

▪▪▪▪

Dr. Lanneman was talking to Dad in front of Mom's room when I came up. He had to talk pretty loud for Dad to hear. Dad was shaking his head.

"I do not understand, Doctor. You said yesterday she was doing better."

"I wouldn't be too discouraged by the change. There is often some instability in response to new insulin."

"Then how can you say she can still come home tonight?"

"Your wife is very unhappy in the hospital, Mr. Witkowski. I believe going home will help her state of mind, which is important to her recovery. Of course, you will have to watch her closely and bring her back if there is any indication of a problem." He glanced at me. "How are you, Lee?"

"Fine, thanks, Dr. Lanneman."

Dad was frowning. "I do not like this. I do not like that she should leave the hospital if she is not doing well."

"Let me make myself clear, Mr. Witkowski. She *is* doing well—just not as well as expected. I want you to take her home where she will be more comfortable, then call me in the morning and we'll see what's what."

Dad waited until Dr. Lanneman was out of

earshot. "You see? You see I am right for you not to play tonight. I knew we will need you. We will take your mother home now, and you will be there to give her shots or bring her back if she gets sick."

"Dad, I—"

"You must always think ahead, Norek. You cannot do whatever you want whenever you want. You have to plan for what might happen, be ready for the worst, always."

"Dad, the guys—"

"I do not like this bringing her home when she is unstable. But you will be there."

"Dad . . . what if something happens that I can't take care of?"

"What could happen?"

"I don't know, and that's the point. What if she's unconscious? What if she doesn't respond to the insulin? What if she responds too much? I'm just a kid. I'm not in medical school yet, not even college. I can't be the one who's responsible."

"Do you say I do not take care of your mother?"

"No, that's not—"

"Good. Because if you do . . ." His face seemed to crumble for an instant; then it hardened back into its familiar frown of disapproval. "If I only could have the opportunity to stay with my mother . . ."

He turned his back to me and went into Mom's room. "Miriam," I heard him say, "you are going home."

I leaned forward, resting my head against the

cool wall. I couldn't make it to the concert if I had to take care of Mom. I shoved my fists deep into my pockets to keep from slamming them into something.

Was that all this was about? Me, playing in a band?

What kind of selfish son was I?

The fingers of my left hand began to play Hendrix's "Castles Made of Sand" against my palm. It was the kind of riff that got inside you so you didn't know you were listening to anything, you just felt the tones flowing, going up and over, bursting through all the words, all the barriers you live with every day, everywhere, the words that keep you tied down, it all dissolves and you fly on the music to someplace different. Someplace open.

Someplace where you can live your own life.

▪▪▪▪

Sounds of packing reached me from Mom's room. She was still in bed when I went in. "Norek," she said, "I am sorry about your concert."

"How are you feeling, Mom?"

"I will be better once I am home. Do you have my clothing, Yosef?"

I was shaking and sweating. "Dad, we could call Stan—"

"He will not come."

"Yes, he will. And he can—"

"Stan will not do this. Only you, Lee."

"But the band—"

"Enough! This band of yours means nothing. Your mother needs you."

"My mother needs . . ." I couldn't finish my sentence. "There's nothing I can do that you or Stan can't, if she gets really sick."

"We will not bother your mother with this nonsense." He handed Mom her clothes and walked out. I followed him to the waiting room.

He pursed his lips in that way I hated, the way that meant he was going to do what he wanted, no matter what. Actually, it meant that *I* was going to do what he wanted, no matter what.

"Your mother will not get really sick," he said. "You will take good care of her. If she gets really sick, you will drive her back here."

My stomach hurt. "If she gets really sick, Dad, you won't need me to drive." I pulled the car keys out of my pocket. "You'll need an ambulance."

Dad stared at me as if I were his enemy. "If you go out tonight, you do not need to come home. You can go into the army, like your brother. Only you won't go to Europe. You will go to Vietnam."

I shut my eyes, and tried to shut out my father by listening to the riffs that always played in my mind. If only I could live in the music and forget all the words.

But his voice boomed like grenades. "If you go out tonight and something happens to your mother, you selfish son, it will be your fault."

The tones in my head began to crash together until they sounded like machine-gun fire. I pictured

Stan in his army uniform. The image of his bulging veins played in my mind. I opened my eyes.

"No, Dad," I said. "It won't."

▪▪▪▪

I called Stan from the hospital; he said he'd be at the house as soon as he could. He wasn't there yet when we pulled into the driveway. Dad helped Mom inside while I got her bags.

She went to bed and fell asleep instantly. I refrigerated the insulin, read the hospital instructions to Dad, and showed him what to do if she needed a shot. If he or Stan put together the right dose, she could probably do the injection herself—that was the part Dad had a hard time with. I left the emergency number near the phone, too, just in case, and set my guitar by the front door.

"You will not go, Lee," Dad tried one last time.

"I have to, Dad. How many chances do you get in a lifetime to play in the Hollywood Bowl?"

"How many mothers do you get in a lifetime?"

I heard Stan's motorcycle pull up then, so I grabbed my stuff and headed out.

"She's asleep," I told him.

He nodded. "Break a leg, kid."

▪▪▪▪

I'm not sure how I got there. I must have followed the traffic laws, since I didn't get a ticket. They'd given me a parking pass as a band member. Handing it to the attendant and pulling into the VIP lot felt so great that for a moment I almost forgot how pale Mom looked when I left.

Backstage, the guys waved me over.

"Cool, man, you made it!" Neil clapped my shoulder.

Elliott nodded. "Mickey's gonna play that one number. Now you're here, we can do the rest, too."

We took our instruments into a soundproof room and tuned up, then waited in the wings for our turn.

When we finally got called on stage, around ten-thirty, I thought I'd died and was facing God. Everything was dark except the white spotlights that shone on us even as we plugged in and checked our tunings. You could smell the smoke from the cigarettes in the crowd, blown onstage by the cool evening breeze wafting around the hot air rising from the amps.

Then came Elliott's voice: "Uh-one and uh-two and . . ."

We did two numbers; then I got the signal to leave, and Mickey came on. I stood in the wings, listening. A man in overalls tapped me on the shoulder.

"Witkowski? You got a call." He nodded to a tiny glass-enclosed office.

It was Stan. "Something's wrong. We're taking her to the hospital. You should probably go there when you're done."

"I'll come right now."

"What good will that do?"

"I'll come home and drive you there."

"You can't get here fast enough. An ambulance is on its way. Finish your set and meet us there."

"Oh. Right. Okay."

Elliott was at the mike. It was as if nothing existed except me and Elliott, and an ambulance somewhere screaming toward my mom. My job was to tell Elliott I had to leave, I knew that, I focused on that, everything else felt numb and far away. I walked onstage—it was just luck that they'd ended the song and I didn't interrupt—and whispered to Elliott that we had to wrap up.

Mickey handed me my guitar as he walked off. Without thinking, I pulled the strap over my head.

"One more?" Elliott asked.

I stared at him. All I could hear was that siren's wail, but it wasn't a siren, it was me playing, my guitar making those high, clear sounds, bending up and pushing off into the next note, and the next, turning them into a melody. I was playing "Castles Made of Sand." Neil picked up the beat, Melnick came in on the bass. Then Elliott added his guitar, but he didn't sing, he just let me carry the song, pulling it along the streets of L.A., wheels screaming across the asphalt, fingers flying over the fret board, into the night where nothing is clear, where sound matters more than sight, pulling the song away from the words and into the music that's always there, waiting in shadows and silence.

I don't know how we got through the number. We'd never played it like that before, without vocals and with me leading off, but somehow we ended it together. I hurried offstage, spotlights whirling behind me.

Elliott followed. “Listen to that. You gotta come back, man.” The audience was yelling and whistling and stamping. “That was great.”

“Yeah” was all I could say. I shoved my guitar into its case. Then I added, “Thanks.”

I raced across the parking lot and slammed the trunk shut over my guitar. Behind me, the spotlights spun crazily as I steered onto the street.

▪▪▪▪

Stan was pacing outside the elevator when I got off at the fifth floor, where they put diabetics. Mom’s floor, as I always thought of it.

His eyes were narrow, his lips tight. He looked so much like Dad that I almost steeled myself against a barrage.

“How is she?” I asked.

“She’ll be okay. At first they thought she wouldn’t pull through, but now they’re saying she’ll make it.”

I nodded, relief flooding through me.

“How’d it go?” Stan asked.

For an instant, I was confused about what he meant. Then I answered, “Good.” I was staring down at the gray pattern on the linoleum floor. “It was good.”

His words echoed through me. At first they thought she wouldn’t pull through, he’d said. My body tightened. My fingers closed into fists.

I looked back at him. "What happened? What was her sugar? Did you give her the right dose?"

"It wasn't like that. We couldn't wake her up. Lanneman says the insulin wasn't working right."

"You mean, while I was playing she might have died?"

"She might have."

I stared at him, not believing he could just say it like that. The elevator rumbled beneath my feet, like applause—people clapping for me while my mother lay dying.

"Dad was right," I heard myself saying. "He was right. I should've been there."

"What good would that have done?"

"Next time will be different. Next time I won't be off playing at a fuckin' rock 'n' roll concert."

Stan's voice was low, his words deliberate. "It wasn't a 'fuckin'' concert, Nate. It was *your* concert."

My concert.

I heard the strains of music again, the riff I'd been playing at the end, my fingers making notes that sailed out of my guitar, past the audience, into the night.

My concert.

My hands loosened; my neck eased—I hadn't realized it was so tight that it was hurting. Air conditioning blew across my face, as cool as the evening breeze at the Hollywood Bowl.

Dad appeared in front of a room down the hall. He looked at us. I couldn't make out his expression, but I could imagine it.

Stan's hand was on my shoulder until I stepped past him and turned to face Dad. "Come on," I said. "Let's go see them."

Together we walked toward Mom's room, the sound of our footsteps echoing like riffs down the hallway, where the odor of medicine can never fully hide the too-sweet smell underneath.

If I didn't have music, I don't know
if I could ever be truly happy.
Happiness is music to me. Like when
I am in Caleb's room, playing
my guitar for him, watching him
close his eyes to listen and knowing
he understands what I am
singing. That is all I need
to make a room full of happiness—
two boys, one love, and a song.

I think the reason my parents wanted me
to play classical music was because
it didn't have any words. They would keep me
as a sound, not a voice. But I had

other ideas. I blew off the recorder,
did not bow to the violin, benched the piano, saved
up for a guitar. Then I used it to write
love songs for boys, and sad songs for love.
I sang myself to find myself
in a language far from my parents'
expectations. I taught myself the strings,
the chords, the fretting. But I did not
have to teach myself the words.
They'd always been there, notes to myself,
waiting for the music to bring them out.

All I had to do was recognize the possibility
of music for the songs to be everywhere.
It is not something I have control over,
no more than I can control the sights
that appear before my eyes. I will be staring off
in class, barely hearing the echo of
my teacher's words, when suddenly
a verse will arrive free-form in my thoughts.

when I look out a window
I wish for you on the other side
even if you're not there
I can see you in the clouds

As I transcribe the words in my notebook,
I can hear the sound of it in my head.
Many teachers have caught me strumming
an imaginary guitar, trying to find the chords
before they vanish with the next thought.

The first time I went out with Caleb,
this happened to me. We were talking
in the park, having a conversation that lasted
the afternoon and the evening,
finding all of our common coincidences,
baring some of our unfortunate quirks.
At one point he went to get us sodas,
leaving me with my thoughts and the trees.
I was elated to have found someone
who could be both interested and interesting.
My thoughts revealed themselves
in the terms of a song.

you could be
the leaf that never falls from the tree
you could be
the sun that never leaves the sky
this might be
the happy ending without the ending
this might be
a reason to try

When he returned to me, he had two bottles
in his hands, and I was making furious leaps
into my notebook, playing the ghost guitar
and singing snatches to the birds around me.
I apologized, embarrassed to be caught
showing him myself so early, but he said
it was charming, then asked me if I needed time
to finish my refrain. Perhaps it's because he
said something so perfect, or perhaps it's because

the song made me brave, but I asked him
if he wanted to hear it, and when he said yes,
I sang to him, accompanied only by
the guitar in my head and the beat
of my heart. When I was done, there was
a moment of absolute silence, and I felt
like the ground had been pulled out from under me
and I was about to fall far. But then the ground
came back as he told me it was wonderful,
as he asked me to sing it to him again.

It is a sad fact of our present times
that it's nearly impossible to turn on the radio
and hear a gay boy with a guitar.
Where are the indigo boys, to show me
the way? Caleb teases me, because while
he has a gay music collection—pop queens
and piano boys—I am, he insists, a closet
lesbian. So I play him some Dylan, some Joni,
some Nick Drake, and I tell him there is
room for me to sing about the two of us
tangled up in blue under a pink
pink pink pink moon. Music, like love,
cannot be defined, except
in the broadest of senses.

My father complains, my mother stays silent.

My father says it's not the music he minds,
but that I play it so loud. They want me
to sing in the basement, but I can't think
with the laundry and the cobwebs—
down there, all my songs begin to have
pipes. So I become a bedroom Cinderella
on a tighter deadline, allowed to sing loud
until the hour hand tips the ten. Then I strum
softly, sing in a whisper.

I think they would like the songs better
if I left out the names, or changed
the pronouns.

No more danger
Time's a stranger
When I'm in his arms
In his arms

He could break me
But instead he wakes me
When I'm in his arms
In his arms

I am not the first person
to avoid the second person.
But I am certainly the first person
to do it in my house.

■■■■

I never thought I would end up with
someone who wasn't possessed
by music in the same way I am.
I imagined a relationship of duets,
of you play me yours and I'll
play you mine. Caleb doesn't
even listen to the music I like. He dances
instead, frees himself that way,
while I prefer the quieter corners,
the blank pages. Part of my music
is being alone, having that time
to shut down all the other noises
to hear the tune underneath.
Sometimes I retreat when he
wants me the most. Sometimes
he wants me the most when I
retreat. I will let the phone ring,
let the IM blink, and he will know
that I am there, not realizing I am
also in another place. I still sing him
songs before I am ready, sing him
back the moments he has missed.
as if to say, *this is where I was*
when you couldn't find me.
The sound of my voice means
I have returned to him, ready
for a different kind of duet,
that delicate, serendipitous pairing
of listened and sung. He accepts that,
and wants more.

black ink
falls on the blue lines
spelling out silences
harboring words

you think
my love's not the true kind
unanswering questions
do not disturb

but I'm not leaving you
when I leave you
I'm not forgetting
that we're getting somewhere
I'm just trying
to figure my part of this
my place in the world
with you standing there

with you standing there...

Our local coffee hangout decides to throw a weekly open mic night. I decide to go as a member of the audience, unsure about playing in a town that knows me unwell. A local band snarls through three songs, then a girl from my school recites poems from a long black book.

I realize I can do this, that I want to be
heard, that it's possible I have something
to say. Word spreads, and all the next week,
my friends tell me to do it, convince me
they'll be there next time. And that is perhaps
the most surprising thing, to feel such support
for this secretive calling. So I sign my name
to the roster, and Caleb makes fliers
on his computer. He slips them into lockers
and strangers from school tell me they'll be there.
Sometimes I've skipped study hall and
practiced in the abandoned stairwell by
the auditorium. Now I'm seeing how many
people have overheard. They have listened in.

I practice past my curfew, past midnight,
into dreamtime. In a moment of weakness,
to fend off their laying down the law, I tell
my parents I have a gig coming up, as if
they would be proud of me singing in public.
My mother, polite, says it sounds nice.
My father tells me it had better not interfere
with my homework. I tell him it won't,
in a voice that's so ready to leave.
Doors do not slam, but they do not stay open
as I sneak music into the house, as I whisper
my longings to the furniture, my fears
to the ceiling, my hopes to the line of
hallway light that goes off beneath my door.

silent night
stay with me
hold me tight
then set me free

daylight will
blind me still
the child's dream
not what it seemed

we search for safer passage
we pray our eyes adjust
we cling to all that's offered
we do what we must

storm outside
thunder warns
deepest fears
since we were born

take me now
show me how
to fight the dark
to find a spark

you are my spark

Who is the *you?* Sometimes when I'm writing I don't know. I am singing out to the stranger of my songs.

■ ■ ■ ■

On Friday, Caleb won't take no for an answer.
We are going out to the club he loves, the one
I've always managed to avoid. He wants to dance,
and he wants me to dance with him. I can't
say no. Even though I dread it, even though
it's not my thing, I will do it for him, because
he has done so much for me. He asks me what
I'm going to wear, and I tell him I was planning
on wearing what I wore to school. He laughs
and tells me to go home and put on something
a little more clubby. For him, this means tighter.
For me, this means darker jeans. When I go home
to change, I don't pick up my guitar, because
I know if I do, I might never leave it.

It's under-18 night at the Continental,
which means there's no drinking,
except for the few hours beforehand.
I carry a small notebook in my back pocket,
although I can't see the music coming to me
here. It is too loud. A singer-songwriter
nightmare. Speakers blasting the *thump-thunk-thump*
of a dance floor mainstay, while the singer belts
the same three lines over and over and over again.
I love this song! Caleb cries, pulling me into
the flashing lights. He looks hot, and everyone else
seems to be noticing. I am lost. It feels like the music
is being imposed on me. I struggle to sway while

Caleb soars. This is his place. This is the liberation
he's found. And there is something beautiful about it,
this closed room where boys slide up to boys
and find a rhythm that defies everything outside.
The music elevates them, takes their cares away
and gives them only one care in return—this movement,
this heat, these lights that turn them into a neon crowd
feverish in their release, comfortable in their bodies
as they leave them in the synthesized rush.
I observe this without feeling a part of it.
Caleb holds me and pulls me into him and I feel
nothing but the ways my body can't move,
the songs inside that are being drowned out
in this rush. Caleb asks *what's wrong* and I say
nothing and keep trying until Caleb senses it again,
says *what's wrong* and this time I know what's
implied—that the something that's wrong
is me. I tell him I need some water, and when I go
he does not follow.

I get some water and stand on the sidelines.
I watch him and don't recognize him
as the boy I have felt love for. He is joyous
in his movements, holding and groping and swaying
in time with his new partner. And I know it's not
that he likes this other boy, I know it's just part of
the dance, but suddenly I am seeing all the things
I will never be able to give him. I am seeing
that I cannot be a part of the music that sets him
free. And it's seeing it in those terms that does it,
that fills me with loneliness. I will stand here

for the rest of the night, and he will dance there.
He has listened to me for hour upon hour, and so
I have dressed the part, I have made the appearance,
I have tried the groove. But in the end he will say
I closed my ears to him, and he will not be wrong.
I take out my notebook, take out my pen,
but the lines remain empty. I cannot think,
I am thinking so much.

For the first time ever, we drive home in silence.
He is sweaty, ragged, angry, beautiful.
I reach out my hand to say I'm sorry.
He takes it, but gives nothing else away.

That night I go to the basement and play loud
enough to wake the neighbors, but not
to wake myself. I once read some guy who said
we listen to songs to figure them out, to unravel
the mystery of the words and tune. I am writing
in order to unravel myself, to find out what
exactly I'm doing, and why.

the windows are closed
but the family's still inside
lighting candles in the blackout
walking by the glow

I'm singing to myself. I'm singing to him.

I am standing on the street
the lamplights are a darkness
I've lost my sense of direction
I have nowhere to go

what do I know?

The next day I return to my bedroom, leaving only for food, and barely any of that. I sing the whole day away, playing the guitar when my voice leaves me, using my desk as a drum when my fingers start to hurt from the strings.

the windows are closed
but I can feel you on the other side
from the dark of my bedroom
you're just out of reach

At midnight I hear someone outside my door, hovering. I yell *GO AWAY* in an ugly voice. The someone goes away without a word, but the hallway light stays on.

I am pressing on the walls
no stars around to guide me
I've lost my sense of direction
falling into the breach

what do I know?

He doesn't call. I know
he is waiting for me to call.
But I don't, and I don't
even know why.

On Sunday my mother finally finds
the courage to stick her head in.
She asks me if everything is okay
and I laugh.

Monday is the night I am supposed to play at
the open mic. I'm ready to abandon it, but
people keep stopping in the halls, telling me
they'll be there. I shouldn't have come
to school. I see Caleb before history and can tell
he's upset, or maybe angry, or maybe both.
He asks me what's going on, and again I use
the least appropriate word, which is
nothing. He asks me if I'm ready
for tonight, and if I still need a ride, and I say no,
and yes. We don't know what to do
with each other, except make plans.

I stay late in the abandoned stairs
by the auditorium, practicing. I'll have
three songs to make an impression,
so I play at least a dozen, trying to figure out
which three. As I sing, I realize
how much I miss him. As if the boy

who wrote the words is reaching
across time to point me back
in the right direction. He's saying
either you were wrong when you wrote this or
you are wrong now. I close my eyes, I sing
a song that was not for a stranger.

When I'm in his arms
I feel that I could fit
In this world
For now
I feel that I could love
This world
For now

No other places
As life embraces
When I'm in his arms
In his arms

and I see him.

There's no song that says what I have to
say to him, but it feels like a song,
in that it is something I must express—
there are words inside of me that I must
release. He picks me up at the school,
his radio blaring, and when I turn it down
he shoots me a look. And I tell him I missed

him. I tell him I missed him when he was
on the dance floor, and in our silence
ever since. I tell him our music doesn't
have to be the same, and he tells me
he already knew this, but wasn't sure
if I ever could. He says he doesn't know
if he could ever make me as happy
as finding the right word, the right bridge,
the perfect refrain. And I tell him that music
cannot be separated from life, that you
can't have one without the other, that
he is my love song as much
as anyone can be. But I am still not sure
that I can be his dance. He parks the car and
kisses me softly and says *this is the dance*
and I kiss him hard and say *this is the song.*
Because all of the chords are in a crescendo
and he is their source.

When I show up at the coffee place, I see
my friends have arrived on time, which is
nothing short of a miracle. It makes me feel
like I belong to something, that somehow
I have drawn these people together to hear me,
because I know they wouldn't be here together
without me. That means so much.
I am the second act on the list, so while
the first singer torches some standards, I make
a quick dive to the restroom. When I emerge,

Caleb is waiting for me. I can see he's nervous
on my behalf, which makes me want to kiss him
again (so I do). He looks surprised, and
before I can ask why, he tells me my mother
is here. And sure enough, I look over his shoulder
and there she is. Without missing a beat, she
waves. I am now nervous on my own
behalf. I ask Caleb what she's doing here,
and he says *I think she's come to see her son sing.*

I hear my name over the low-grade speakers.
I hear the cappuccino machine burping
behind the counter, the sound of mugs
settling on formica, the murmur of strangers.
I stand up on the makeshift stage, really just

an area where the tables have been cleared away.
When I look to my side, I can see Caleb
standing right there. And when I look to
the makeshift audience, I see my mother there,
a table to herself, nervous, too, and proud.

I tune for a moment and realize the song
I need most is the one I've just finished,
the one I played all weekend.

the windows are closed
but the family's still inside
lighting candles in the blackout
walking by the glow

I am standing on the street
the lamplights are a darkness
I've lost my sense of direction
I have nowhere to go

what do I know?

As I sing to Caleb, I know that this song is
no longer about us. Or if it's about us,
it's not about now. I turn to my mother
as I hit the refrain

when you hear me
listen to what I'm saying
when you see me
look me in the eye
when you know me
try not be frightened
when you speak to me
tell me everything
is going to be fine

and the most astonishing thing happens,
which at first I can't believe—
my mother, in her own quiet way,
is singing along.

Her mouth is moving with mine, she knows
all the words. I am almost thrown from
the second verse, because I am realizing how

deaf I have been. I have misinterpreted the footsteps in the hallways. I have not seen or listened or known. And I am near tears, looking at Caleb, looking at my mother, because for a boy who has been spending all his time on music, it's not until now that I know what a song can do. The second refrain switches a little, but my mother knows that. We are looking right at each other and we are singing to the end

when you know me
try not be frightened
when you see me
look me in the eye
when you hear me
listen to what I'm saying
when you speak to me
tell me everything
is going to be fine

it's going to be fine

the windows are closed
so we stumble to the doors
follow the sound of my voice
saying everything
is going to be fine

At first I don't understand the applause, because that's not where I am. I am making a new song

out of my mother's expression, the devotion
I've been too slow to notice, and Caleb's music,
the dancing that we'll do.

This is what a song can do. Our moments are
music, and sometimes—just sometimes—
we can catch them and put them
into some lasting form. If I didn't
have music, I don't know if
I could ever be truly happy,
and if I didn't have these moments,
I would never find music. It is everywhere,
in the air between us, waiting
to be sung.

For me, the piano is a person. Rania, my friend at a UN-run refugee girls' school in Ramallah, introduced me to it. Rania was one of five Christian students in my school. The rest of us girls were Muslims. During religion class, she had the option of having free time or studying Islam with us.

Rania did not like to study. She liked to draw. The pages in her notebooks were tiny paintings, with few notes. She wanted to grow up and marry someone who would take her to live in America. She had many relatives there. They sent her gifts, clothes, lots of American candy that she offered to share with me. In return I would help her with homework, especially algebra.

Algebra was a magical subject for me. Our math teacher had explained that it was invented by

Al-Khawarizmi, a Muslim man who was born in Iran and lived in Baghdad for a long time. He wrote his books in Arabic. He developed algebra to solve the practical questions of people in issues of inheritance and commerce. He meant to treat and mend the fractions of numbers, as one restores broken bones. I felt proud to write the same language as Al-Khawarizmi, whom I called Rizmi in my imaginary conversation with him as I did my homework. I cared to restore fractions as he did.

I imagined Rizmi might have looked like my father. But I wanted to make up for my father, who could not read or write except the basics. He could not invent a discipline like algebra. My father had finished first grade only.

Algebra was the Arabic candy for my mind. I dissolved the problems, solved them, no matter how complex they were. When the teacher said that being able to solve math problems could train our minds to solve complex issues, I thought of the problem between Israel and Palestine, and wanted to learn more math because of it. I wanted to know all about geometry, modern math, anything that trained my mind to solve a problem that had divided our land, subtracted lives daily, added mounds of pain, multiplied fear, and left us fragmented. A solution must be derived, the bones of our world restored.

"Music is also mathematical," our teacher added. "Think about it; playing the drum, the oud, the flute, and the piano are all mathematical." I was surprised to hear this.

It seemed to me that most Palestinian homes had a tablah, a dumbek drum. I had heard drumming often, heard it during summer nights, at times played slowly with beats as round and heavy as elephant footsteps, and at others played in a rush, fingers light as a feather, quick as lightning. I thought the sky was pouring rain. When I heard it played with a lulling pulse, I could see why the heart beats also. I had danced to the drum till my feet could dance no more, but I had not thought of it as math. There was no problem there to solve other than how to wake up early the following day.

The oud, the Arabic lute, also lived in many Palestinian homes. I had known the oud to tear up the heart with its tunes. But its six strings could simultaneously stitch it back together into a purse of ecstasy. In Palestine, the oud sound is like a call for prayer of a different kind. It can drive a Palestinian toward the divine. At the end of an oud night, a person becomes momentarily peaceful amid war. I knew the oud was magical, but never thought it mathematical.

And I had heard the shabbabeh, a flute, played by shepherds on hills. They whistled and the echo traveled into valleys, returned, and formed a multi-layered wind ensemble to play with them. Their sheep ate music when they could not find grass.

But the piano I had seen only in pictures. There were no pianos in refugee camps. The wish to touch a piano tortured me. I told Rania, but I did not realize that she would be the one to solve this problem. "I can show you one, in the flesh and blood," she said.

The church where Rania and her family worshiped had a piano. Rania's father was the church's guard. He let us in excitedly when she explained that I helped her with homework.

That was the first time in my entire life I had entered a church. The seats were long. One could sleep on them. The room was large; many camp families might be able to fit in it. The tall glass was crowdedly colorful with geranium red, molasses brown, spearmint green, iris purple—colors that soothed the spirit. The walls were painted with pictures of people and angels. Rania pointed to the largest: "Al-Maseeh," she said. Messiah.

"And I am Reem." I introduced myself to the picture. Rania liked my respect for her world.

Rania led me to an elephant-sized piano that squatted serenely in a corner of the church. Before I touched the piano, the sight of it touched me. It reminded me of the first and only time I had visited a zoo. I twirled with delight.

A notebook filled with lines and bead-sized dots had been left open. "These are notes. One can read them like numbers in a math book. They translate to phrases, passages, long songs," she explained.

Songs? Now the beads became birds on the page, long rows on electric wires, singing. Was it possible that these beads could really sing like birds? What must I do to make them do it?

"Open the lid," she said. A large number of black and white teeth smiled at me. I became more excited, happy, afraid, all at once. The lid was more of a lip. And I instantly knew why the piano might sing, why the notes could be more than a row of birds. The piano could be a person who loves numbers.

Rania's father came over to watch us. He noticed the stunned look on my face. "You don't have to read the beads. Just sit down; play the keys." I remained reluctant. "There are no rules for playing," he explained. "You don't have to make songs. Just make music." He shut the bead book.

"There are no teachers here. This is not a school," he encouraged. "I am a church guard. I did not finish my schooling because I didn't like homework or teachers. Just play like a child would."

I raised a finger as though it were a foot about to enter a new world. I dipped my finger onto a white bar. I dipped other fingers. All dropped inside a sweet, liquid sound. The white and black might have been sugar wafers, or chocolate bars for a person's ears. I licked my fingers.

Rania and her father applauded. A thrill of importance ran through me. I had touched a piano, unlike most refugee-camp children, and tasted its music. I had also entered a church, all in an hour.

I came to the church every day after school. Other girls thought about boys, but I thought about a piano. Songs ran in my mind nonstop, like hamsters on wheels. My life began to have a sound track that made me dance in steps and skips as I composed it. I integrated the fragments of my thoughts into notes that made me cry when they finally met.

I closed my eyes and touched the piano. I told it my secrets; it broke them down into sounds. I told it the equations of life I could not understand. The piano simplified the stories bracketed in my heart; it turned them into simple notes, echoing with the possibility of solutions. It solved for *y*. I understood its explanations.

And I imagined the keys of the piano leading to doors, the doors leading to rooms where the sound slept lonely, untouched, and frozen as a prisoner. The keys were in my hands. I turned them. I set the sound free, let it escape its silence.

No one knew it, but with the piano I had come out of the crowd of life to listen to myself. Images from the hungry life at the camp, angry sounds of street confrontations with soldiers, splinters of the stories refugees carried silently in themselves, all surfaced in the grand silences between the sounds. I kept my fingers singing.

As it listened, the piano made my life more equal to what I had hoped it would be. It became my playground, with notes flat as pastures I ran into, notes sharp as mountains I climbed up, and phrases spoken from atop mountains. The piano repaired my days like a sewing machine repairs a dress.

One day, when students were let out from

school early because the city was filled with demonstrations, I decided to play the piano before returning home.

Inside the church, as I lifted the lip of the piano to let it speak to me, I could hear the drums of a demonstration nearing. The chanting that accompanied that drumming stirred a deep quickening of fear in me. I knew the songs. I knew the stories behind them. And I knew that most demonstrations did not pass peacefully. I could visualize the bright green of the Palestinian flag flying, momentarily, until the khaki green of the soldiers arrived and pulled it to the ground.

I wanted to go home. But within moments the roads would be closed down, and my home was on the other side of town. The call for a curfew was repeated through loudspeakers. Anyone seen on the streets would be shot down, or beaten up, taken to prison. I heard bullets being fired.

Rania's father and I stood at the door of the church to decide what we should do. He said the church was a safe place, but that he was not going to stay in it. He had a small room a few yards away where he spent the night at times—times like this. I could stay with the piano if I wanted to. But I must shut the door until things had calmed down.

I chose to stay with the piano, and agreed to call to Rania's father if I needed help. I was about to shut the door, to have the entire muraled room to myself and the piano, when a boy erupted from the street and ran inside. His eyes searched for a dark place. He saw the piano at once and ran to it. He disappeared from the room like a pebble inside a lake. The room returned to its quiet.

Rania's father whispered that the boy must be escaping from soldiers. "They are likely to follow in moments," he added. He and I stood at the door, fear flying off our shoulders as sparrows.

The soldiers arrived. Rania's father said I was his daughter and that we were guarding the church. He invited them to search inside. The soldiers were hesitant to enter, perhaps because the church was an unfamiliar, closed-off place. They warned that it was our responsibility to not let anyone enter. Cradling their guns in their arms like babies, they turned their backs and returned to the streets.

Behind the piano, the boy had gathered up his body into a mound. His skin and hair were brown, dark like mine. His knees were tucked into his chest; his arms tight around him. He seemed a wounded bird, broken somewhere, but he would not speak of it. With a gesture from his eyes, he asked that I not inspect his body with my gaze.

I returned to the piano. I sat down. I spoke to the boy without looking at him. If anyone suddenly entered the room, they would think I was singing.

"You don't have to answer my questions," I said. "But I want to ask you. Whose son are you?" In Palestine most people know one another by family name. The boy did not answer. "What is your name?" Still he did not answer. "Are you afraid like

I am?" He cleared his throat but did not speak. "Have you touched a piano before?" He gave no answer. "Could I play it for you? It would take away our fears, I promise."

He said yes.

I felt hope fill me. I wanted to make the keys speak, open up their mouths, scream a solution. When my fingers touched the keys, they spoke to me. They reminded me that simply telling one's story to ears that listen can be medicine.

I invited the boy to speak. My hands began to compose a sound track for his story. Faintly, and for many minutes, my left hand played the drum leading the demonstrators. I wanted to stay there, inside the warmth of the drum, but the beat was broken. The soldiers arrived with the screeching sound of their jeeps, a menace. Then came the confrontation, chaos. I stomped on the piano with my fingers, slapped its face. I wanted a different outcome for this problem.

Then I entered sadness. My fingers made stroking sounds as long as streets. And suddenly I wished the piano were a beast that would leap out of the room, carrying the boy in its lap, and cross the city to where his mother was. Son plus mother equals safety: that's the solution I truly wanted.

"Tell me what happened to you today?" I asked.

"Five soldiers beat me up with clubs. I cannot feel my body," he answered, his words fighting to be heard. "I cannot feel my body." He cried quietly.

One divided by five. That's a weak chance for

one person not to be fractured. I wanted to embrace the boy, but all I could do was play an embrace of sounds. I had been sternly instructed by my mother that a Muslim girl must not touch boys who are not close family members.

"Keep on playing this," he whispered. He sobbed as though I touched his wounds. "Keep on playing this." I played until he became quiet again. He said he wanted to sleep. I gave him my math book for a pillow.

He put his head on the book filled with problems I could solve in my sleep. But now I was wide awake, feeling defeated, paralyzed. My mind was numb with the pain I felt rising like steam from the boy's body behind the piano.

I looked at the silent painting of the Messiah. He came as a solution. He was Palestinian, born in Bethlehem, where many of Rania's relatives live; yes, and he was a Jew. Perhaps the math of the Middle East does not extend beyond the number one, and we are all fractions of it.

I thought of Rizmi. I realized that he had a hopeful mind. I liked him more. Most problems in the discipline he had invented have solutions. Some equations have infinite solutions, though a few have none.

What might he think? I wondered. Perhaps he would simplify the problem by solving for hope in each person's mind, and would solve for tears that would void our pain and anger. The love would remain; we would live like the black and white keys of a piano, a numerator equal to a denominator. Even when divided by conflict, our outcome would be One. The Messiah would agree with Rizmi.

The boy spoke again. "Could you play as I sleep?" he asked. "Do you know a lullaby?" I did not know any lullabies or children's songs except for one about a chicken that goes to the market and buys something for her mother. I had never played it before on the piano. But at the boy's request, the tune came into my mind full, like a moon. My fingers turned into magnets that pulled out the notes and prayed the pain would be pulled out of the boy's body.

He fell asleep, on the floor. He had refused to move from behind the piano. The lullaby tune covered him like a blanket. I slept on a long wooden seat till the morning, when Rania's father called through the door that the curfew had been lifted.

I ran to the boy. He was still curled up. But now I could see that a thin line of blood had run out of his nose and dried on his lip. I touched his hand. The boy had departed his body. His soul had trickled out with the darkness, step by step, half step by half step—a skip, a leap home to where the muse of all music is.

I stood up, wanted to walk, but felt too weak to carry the story. I leaned on the piano, looked into its face. It stood by me, wide open, ready to embrace me, a person.

Spring Audition Time

The Philharmonic Youth Orchestra will be auditioning young musicians for its world-renowned program on April 1st at the Unitarian Church on Maple Street.

The orchestra, which plays at many local events, also has a sister-city arrangement with a youth orchestra in Leipzig, Germany, the home of Mendelssohn and Bach. The upcoming year will be a touring year for the orchestra, the trip taking them to Paris, France, and cities in Germany, as well as Prague, Bucharest, and a final stop in Moscow.

Funds for the extensive summer travel will be raised by local performances by the full orchestra as well as chamber groups who play for events in the area.

> Wilshire is lucky enough to have such a talented orchestra primarily because of its dedicated leadership, Mr. Paul Smith, Ph.D. Formerly a soloist with the Philadelphia Symphony Orchestra, Mr. Smith has toured the world, playing everything from Vivaldi to Paganini with all the major orchestras. He now is a guest conductor with frequent invitations, but his heart is here in Wilshire: "I'd give anything for my kids," he says. "Sparking the fire of music in their hearts gives meaning to my life."

Cameron put the newspaper down and gulped the rest of her orange juice, hoping it might cool her pounding heart. There was no reason to be nervous. It was the sixth time she had auditioned for Mr. Smith. She'd been in the orchestra for four years already. She had started in the back of the second violins, playing music that was almost too hard for her, and then, year by year, had moved up. This year she was in the first violin section, sixth chair back. She shared a stand with Peter; he was on the outside. Elias was fourth chair, sitting in front of them. The first three chairs were all held by graduating seniors. That meant their chairs were up for grabs. In particular, the concertmaster was leaving.

The first violin of the orchestra is the place of highest honor. The concertmaster is the one who stands up and asks the oboe for the A to tune the orchestra. He plays the solos, with the swelling music of the entire orchestra behind him. This next year, the seat would go to either Peter or Elias. Or to her.

Both Peter and Elias were more talented than she was. She knew that, knew it so well she could spit. She practiced twice as long as they did to get the same notes under control. But neither of them could want the position more than she did. Especially Elias. He only played violin to please his parents, who felt, and rightfully so, that such an extraordinary talent should not go to waste.

Elias was playing the Bach *Double Concerto* when he was six. His fingers didn't have to go through his brain to move fast, they just moved, and always hit the right notes. Elias could get away with not practicing, and Cameron was sure he blew off his orchestra music more often than not. Sometimes he'd fudge a bowing because he just wasn't paying attention. During breaks, he liked to hang out with a trombone player and a drummer, Seth and Paul, and play a fantasy card game. He hid behind his curtain of long dark hair and brooded over his cards. He never had to put in an extra ten minutes on a tricky run of notes like Cameron often did.

Peter loved to play. He played for the fun of it. He slouched into his violin, and with his blond buzz cut and massive arms, he looked more like an athlete, the violin a little stick of wood. He was an athlete, and a good one, too—soccer in the fall, skiing in the winter, soccer again in the spring. But his fingers were long and thin, and he could play notes that ripped like lightning. He played violin because it was easy for him—easy to make music, easy to impress, easy to get attention. He didn't like to work hard, and he didn't care if he made mistakes.

Mr. Smith could not tolerate mistakes. Cameron didn't make mistakes. Cameron practiced for endless hours so that she didn't make mistakes. That was why there was a chance she might get to be concertmistress. She was not a total natural, never would be. But there was a chance, if she worked really hard . . . for the next three days.

She slammed her hand on the table. "Give it up now," she said out loud. Three days was not enough time.

"Give up what?" asked her mother, rubbing the shower water out of her hair.

"Oh, nothing," Cameron said.

Her mother saw the article lying on the table. "You want to be concertmaster next year," she said, smiling.

Cameron closed her eyes and sighed. She knew what her mother was going to say, and it was one thing if she said it to herself, but something totally different if her mother said it to her.

"Just play from your heart." Her mother had said this a million times. "Competing with Elias and Peter is like wrestling a tornado. They are forces of nature. What you've got going for yourself is your love of the music. There is no point in trying to be better than those two. Just play for yourself."

Is it so bad to want to be the best for once? Cameron wanted to say. But instead she sighed, shoved in the chair, and went to her room to get her backpack for school. She grabbed her violin and took off. "I've got a lesson after school," she said as she went out the door; her mother's cheerful good-bye was lost in the slam.

▪▪▪▪

Cameron's teacher, Penelope Redford, was third chair in the first violin section of the Philadelphia Symphony Orchestra. She was one of the best violinists around, but she still was third best. She understood completely how Cameron felt.

"You just can't let your desire tighten up your bow hold," she said. "Loose, loose—there you go—and listen for the ringing tones. Really pull the ring out of the string. Milk it. Get your violin to sing for you."

Cameron was working on Vivaldi's *Four Seasons*. She was going to play the Allegro from "Winter" for the audition, and getting all the double-stops to be exactly in tune was tricky. She had to have two fingers on two strings in the right places so that the notes not only resonated with each other, but with the other strings on the violin. What makes a violin sound so magical, Penelope always said, was that the very wood of the instrument vibrates when the notes are perfectly in tune.

"Play the fast parts accelerated," Penelope said, writing down notes on Cameron's practice sheet. "It's in 3/8, so it's quick already. The eighth note is supposed to be played at 144. Speed it up one notch to at least 152. Then, when you bring it back down, those thirty-second notes will sound easy."

Sure, Cameron thought. But it will be impossible to play them that fast. She could barely get them out at 132.

"Take this home with you and listen," Penelope said, giving Cameron a CD as she packed up her violin. "For inspiration."

▪▪▪▪

Her violin lesson usually left Cameron happy, filled with the energy of the music and Penelope's infectious enthusiasm. But today, as Cameron walked down the tree-lined streets toward home, her mood was as gray as the clouds that threatened to break open in a sodden spring shower. Even the tulips and daffodils looked dreary, their heads drooping for lack of sun. Why, Cameron wondered, had she chosen Vivaldi's "Winter"? Winter was nearly over. She was sick of winter. Maybe she should have done "Summer" instead, or at least "Spring."

She wasn't going to play all of "Winter," just the third movement, just the Allegro. It starts out so mysteriously, the notes curling like wood smoke around the theme. She loved that eerie beginning. But then, the way a sudden blizzard of snow erases the world, the notes take off, skittering all over the place. When the storm passes, the music slows down again, with the feeling that everything is covered in heaps of snow in the deep silence of winter. Then, without warning, the music explodes—

doors open and kids run from their houses in bright snow clothes to go sledding down a hill, screaming with delight, the notes flying with the speed of light on an ice-cold day.

And that's it. It leaves you there, filled with joy.

That's why she was doing it. She loved it.

But there was no point to doing it at all if she couldn't do it well. She might as well just play Bach or something. Something at a decent tempo. Something she knew by heart and could play backward if she wanted to. Something she wouldn't mess up.

She kicked at a beer can that someone had thrown in the street. It made a satisfying clunk. She kicked it all the way home, then brought it in to the recycle bin. Then she got out her violin to practice. Thirty-second notes at 152 for the eighth note. Right. No problem.

After forty minutes of playing the same thirty-six notes up to speed, she still didn't have it fast enough. Her shoulder was clenched, her hand was cramping, and her heart was crushed. She put her violin away. She resisted slamming the case, but she shut it hard enough that the CD that Penelope had given her slipped out of its zippered pocket. Cameron picked it up and went to her room. She lay back on her bed, headphones on, and pressed PLAY. She let the tears pour down her cheeks. She was just not good enough.

Slowly she started listening to the sounds coming into her ears. The music was searing. She felt burned, listening to it. The tears kept flowing, but now they were for the beauty of the music, not for feeling sorry about her lack of talent. Whatever this piece was, she had to learn to play it. She picked up the case, expecting to read about another kid violinist who blew away the world at age fourteen. But the liner notes were about the music. The only thing they said about the musician was that she had started playing violin as an adult and had put together her own orchestra.

Wow. Cameron sat up and dried her face. That was amazing. How could someone play like that if she had never played as a child? How could she just ignore the whole hierarchy of the established orchestras, put together her own, then go and play the music she loved? What a concept.

Cameron took off the headphones and stood by her window. She decided something then, looking out at the rain that was starting to pour. She decided that she was not going to play for anyone other than herself, and if she didn't get concertmaster, she wouldn't care. She would play for the music. She went back downstairs and practiced until she'd nailed the notes, then went on to the next set. She practiced and practiced until the notes became no more than nerve impulses in the tips of her fingers.

▪▪▪▪

Mr. Smith sat in his chair, looking rather severe.

Cameron nervously checked how tight her bow was. It was fine.

Mr. Smith looked at her audition form. "How fast are you taking it?" he asked.

"One forty-four," she said, her voice breaking.

"Up to tempo," he said. "Good for you." He sounded doubtful. "Do you want me to give you the beat?"

Cameron shook her head. "I think I've got it," she said.

And she did. She played it flawlessly. Her arm was loose; her bow sank into the string, drawing out the tones on the slow, wandering part; and her fingers skipped without thinking when the notes got fast. It was as perfect as she could make it. She let the sound float into the room before taking her violin down.

Mr. Smith nodded, not even giving her the reassurance of a smile. Then he stood up and opened a book on her music stand. "Sight-reading," he said.

Cameron's breath froze in her mouth. How could she have spaced it out? Of course there was a note-reading section, there always was. But she had been so worried about the Vivaldi that she had completely forgotten to prepare for this.

It was in 6/8 time. It had four sharps. So it was in the key of . . . E major? Unless it was minor. A third down from E was . . .

"When you are ready," Mr. Smith said.

She just started. It was minor. Something minor. It had tricky held notes and syncopation. She stumbled her way through, her face growing hotter and hotter as she made mistakes. How could she be so stupid?

"Thank you," she said when the torture was over. She stood with her back very straight to leave the room. She was not getting the seat, there was no question.

Peter was out there waiting, wearing a T-shirt with the sleeves rolled up. He hadn't even dressed for the audition. He'd probably just come from soccer.

"Hey, Cameron," he said with a grin. "How was it?"

Cameron grimaced at him.

"Now I'm worried," Peter said, mockingly. He grabbed his violin by the neck like it was some kid dinosaur toy, not a four-thousand dollar instrument, and went into the audition room.

She found her case in the practice room, and contemplated quitting as she put her violin away. It would be another week before they got the letter, but there was no point holding her breath. She knew already.

▪▪▪▪

Orchestra rehearsal was on Saturday morning. The seniors were restless; they were so excited to be almost out of school. They had an air of adulthood about them, as if they had already crossed the border psychologically and had only to step out the door to make it official. Cameron didn't even look up at Mr. Smith. But when Peter came in, he winked at her. She leaned over to ask, "How'd it go?"

"What?" he said, still beaming. Couldn't he take anything seriously?

"The audition, stupid."

"Okay. But the sight-reading was a joke."

"Could you play it?"

"No way. He was just trying to scare us. You know how he is."

"Well, it sure scared me."

Peter laughed, and Cameron felt a bit better.

The concertmaster stood to ask for an A, and the sounds from the orchestra abruptly switched from chattering kids to tuning instruments.

■■■■

The letter was in the pile of mail. It sat there on top, cream-colored and elegant. Cameron didn't even want to touch it, for fear it would bite her. She took it to her room, lay back on the bed, and opened it.

Dear Miss Jimenez,

Thank you so much for your participation in this year's Youth Orchestra auditions. It was obvious that each student invested a great deal of time preparing him- or herself for the event.

My usual practice would be for this letter to announce your acceptance in the orchestra, and to let you know which chair you will be seated in. However, this year the competition was too close for me to make the call.

As a result, I have decided to issue a challenge.

If you would be willing to participate, I would like to invite our top three violinists to engage in a play-off before a live, paying audience. The audience will evaluate the performances and, by voting, choose the concertmaster for next year. A group of local musicians have agreed to accompany you with orchestral music for your solos.

If you would like to engage in this entertaining audition, please choose three pieces of solo violin music: one adagio, one allegro, and one of your choice. Notify my office with your decision by April 15th. The competition will be held on Friday, the 10th of June.

Respectfully yours,
Paul Smith, Director

Cameron was stunned. She didn't know what to think. She read the letter again, and then once more, to see if it had any clues for her. Her brothers were in the living room, jumping on each other, so she went out to the kitchen to phone Penelope. Her mom was chopping onions.

"Penelope, hello. Do you know about this?"

"About the audition? Paul Smith asked me to be in the orchestra."

Cameron paused. "Should I agree?" she asked. Her mother was tapping her shoulder to ask what was up. She handed her mother the letter, as she listened to Penelope.

"I think you have to. The worst you could get is third chair, and that's what you'll get if you don't audition."

"But if I blow it, I'll be in front of hundreds of people."

"Then don't blow it. It's a great idea for a fund-raiser. Besides, it will get the town more personally involved with the orchestra if they have a hand in choosing the concertmaster."

"Or mistress."

Penelope laughed. "When you come for your lesson tomorrow, we'll discuss what music to play."

▪▪▪▪

At orchestra rehearsal, the tension was a little tight when Mr. Smith announced his brilliant idea for the play-off. "I expect you all to be there," he said. "You can have a voice in choosing your leader."

Peter groaned. Cameron hid her face in her hands. Elias just looked out to the empty seats in the audience. He couldn't care less, it seemed.

"Do we have to pay to get in?" asked one of the horns.

"Of course," said Mr. Smith. "And bring your parents. This is the Moscow leg of our trip next year."

A horn player said, "We better not play too fast there, or we'll be rushin.'"

The orchestra groaned, simultaneously and in tune.

Cameron sat beside Peter, with Elias right in front of them. This was the order, by rights. Elias, Peter, and then Cameron. The three of them knew it. Why did they have to present it to the entire town? Elias had a tight frown on his face as he played the Saint-Saëns. Cameron could see him out of the corner of her eye. His father was one of the parents who stayed through every rehearsal, working on his laptop in the back of the room. Elias was lucky to have such devoted parents, Cameron thought. Her mom and dad were busy with her younger brothers, so they pretty much left her to manage her own schedule. If it was really cold or pouring rain, they'd give her a ride, but she mostly walked. It made her feel a bit lonely, when she thought of it. Maybe if she was concertmaster, they'd pay more attention to her music.

They had sixteen measures' rest. Peter leaned over and whispered, "I'm gonna whip your butt." He was grinning.

Cameron decided to not get angry, but it took a conscious decision, like turning a switch firmly off. She could let him win or she could fight him. By measure fourteen, she'd made a decision. "Not on your life," she said, then tucked her violin under her chin and raised her bow.

■ ■ ■ ■

Cameron held the program in her hand. It was printed on heavy, cream-colored paper with their school photos reproduced on the front. The theater was sold out, but people were still standing around, talking excitedly. Cameron stood backstage in the wings, flexing her fingers to keep them warm and trying to remember how to breathe. She was first up, opening with her adagio. Good. She got to start out slow. Slow was hard, but she was really good at it. The orchestra was tuning. There must have been twenty teachers out there, many of them members of the Philadelphia Symphony. She looked at the program again. After her came Elias, with his allegro, then Peter with his adagio. She skimmed the rest of the program. Her Vivaldi was second to last, with Elias playing something she'd never heard of to finish the concert.

Penelope came over to check on Cameron. Since Penelope was acting concertmaster for the night, she was still backstage, waiting to enter. She put her arm around Cameron's shoulder. "How are you doing?" she asked quietly.

Cameron nodded. Penelope rubbed her shoulder muscles. "Keep it soft," she said. "Pull the sound right from your heart. You'll do beautifully."

The lights in the house dimmed. There was a sudden rustle as people sat down and then a hush. Mr. Smith, resplendent in a tuxedo with tails, took Penelope by the arm to escort her to center stage. The audience clapped; she took a bow, then turned to tune with the orchestra.

Mr. Smith explained the voting procedure to the audience. Then he tapped his stand and it was Cameron's turn to walk out, under the lights, to the sound of applause. It sounded like breaking glass. She was terrified.

She was playing the Adagio from Mozart's B-Minor Concerto for Violin and Orchestra. The introduction was long, and the musicians behind her were splendid. Slowly Cameron's self-consciousness fell away and she was able to relax so that when she lifted her bow, she was just an instrument for Mozart's wonderful music to play through. When she had sections where she was playing alone, she could feel the acoustics of the fabulous music hall amplifying her sound, encouraging her to slow down and sink her weight into the bow. The confidence of the orchestra behind her was palpable. She played well, and the applause was tremendous.

She bowed and left. Elias was standing there, his face closed, hiding behind his hair. He didn't even look at her. "Good luck," she whispered, but he didn't answer.

Peter punched her shoulder. "Good job," he said.

"Thanks."

The orchestra began. Elias was playing Kreisler. It was a perfect piece for him, intellectual, precise, and wicked fast. He dug his bow into the string, and the force of his playing was fierce. His hair tossed with the music. He looked the part of the eccentric genius. Cameron couldn't see how his fingers could go that fast. Even the slower lyrical section in the middle was driven. She looked at

Peter. His eyebrows were pressed together. He was annoyed, she could tell, that his first piece was slow and he had to wait to prove that he could go just as fast as Elias. He could, too. The music was taking off again. It made her nervous just to hear it.

The audience burst out clapping.

"Whup him," Cameron said into Peter's ear. Her words seemed to calm the storm on his face.

He smiled at her. "Okay," he said. "I will." He strode out there, even before Elias was completely off the stage. Peter tucked his violin under his chin. He was so big that the instrument looked too small for him, as if he might break it. He nodded to the conductor. When he started to play, the violin grew with its own life, and Peter's body, moving with the music, became part of the instrument. It was amazing to watch.

Elias was pacing around, his violin clutched under his arm. He caught Cameron staring. For a moment his face closed up again, but then he let go of a wash of feelings: pride, frustration, ambition. Cameron knew them all. She touched his arm and said, "Great job."

Elias nodded. It was his way of saying thank you.

Peter was playing something beautiful, and he was playing it beautifully.

Elias stood close behind her, and they listened together. After a moment Elias whispered something. His mouth was right over her shoulder, so he could speak to her without being overheard. "It would be easier if I wanted it," he said.

Cameron stood up straighter, surprised. Her shoulder bumped his chin, but he didn't move.

"What do you want?" she whispered.

"To compose. I just want to write music. But not this ancient classical crap."

Cameron pulled her head back to look at him. He was a little taller than she was, and his hair, tucked behind his ears now, framed his face like a cape. His face had such an intense expression; it was beautiful, or frightening.

"I can't stand it," Elias said, his voice almost inaudible. "Hear that? Peter blew that entire run. He missed the first note, and it screwed him up."

Cameron hadn't noticed. Now she listened to Peter. The music had slowed down again, and he was moving with it, his arms holding his violin and his bow as if they were wings and he was flying, and the wind over the strings was making the music. If he knew he made a mistake, he would never let it show, he was so totally into the performance.

Applause. Elias was up next.

The concert continued with Cameron and Peter playing fast pieces, and Elias a stunning slow movement. They took an intermission before the last set. These were the pieces they had been free to choose. Peter led off with a Seitz concerto. He breezed through it, missing notes here and there, but again performing for the delight of it. He took it way too fast, but the orchestra kept up, and despite his mistakes he had the audience amazed with his virtuosity.

Cameron followed with her Vivaldi "Winter." It was so incredible to play it with the orchestra going *jya-jya-jya-jya* right behind her, giving her a fence to climb on with her notes. Right in the beginning, though, she played a wrong note, and she obsessed about it for a few measures. A mistake. She didn't make mistakes. That was her only hope. She might as well give up.

But then the music began to take over and she disappeared. She lost her thinking brain and became more than the individual notes—she became the flow of notes, the intervals that resonated long after the notes were played. When the fast part came, she danced it; her fingers flew, knowing just where to go. The orchestra flew behind her, building the music to such a crescendo that when she was done the audience exploded, first with silence, then with wild clapping. It was great.

Elias came on as she left the stage. "This piece I wrote myself," he said into the microphone. "It is unaccompanied."

The orchestra sat back in their chairs; the audience sat forward.

His music was different than anything Cameron had ever heard. It was eerie at times, creepy; he played all over the violin, screeching high and moaning down low on the G-string. In the middle there was a surreal bit that wandered around very fast in sixth position and sounded like fairies dancing, Cameron thought, but it was followed by ogres growling and scratching down low. When he was done, he took a bow. The audience clapped as if they weren't sure whether they were supposed to like it or not. One or two people shouted "Bravo!" But it wasn't clear whether they were impressed with his age or with his music. Then Mr. Smith had the three of them come up for a bow, and the audience rose to a standing ovation. Someone came on stage and handed each of them an armful of flowers, and then it was over.

The audience mingled, having hors d'oeuvres and drinks while volunteers collected ballots and tabulated the votes. The three violinists stood together near the buffet table. Elias and Peter kept reaching over for more food. Cameron's stomach felt like a stretched E-string. She couldn't imagine eating.

"You wrote that piece?" Peter asked Elias.

Elias nodded. He looked nervous, as if the idea of playing his own piece was fine but it hadn't occurred to him that he might have to talk about it afterward.

"That was pretty daring."

Then Elias grinned. "I know," he said. "It cost me the seat."

Cameron smiled at him. "I thought it was amazing."

Elias wrinkled up his eyebrows, as if he didn't believe her. "Really?"

Cameron smiled wider. "Yes. And I even liked parts of it."

That made Elias laugh, and with that laugh something shifted. The competition was over. They were no longer against one another.

Peter said, "Well, whoever gets first chair, we'll have to promise to be sick once a month so the other two can take a turn being concertmaster."

▪ ▪ ▪ ▪

Paul Smith, looking smooth in his tuxedo, went up to the stage again, where someone had set up a podium with a microphone. The room hushed. "What a splendid performance tonight by our three promising musicians," he said. "I was particularly thrilled to hear the new piece composed by Elias Levy. It showed the extraordinary musical sensitivity he has developed. I am hopeful that he will compose a piece for this orchestra.

"Furthermore, I think not a single person was left unmoved by the virtuosity and skill displayed by Peter Dawson. His music left many of us breathless.

"But now is the moment we have been waiting for. May I introduce to you all the new concertmistress of the Wilshire Philharmonic Youth Orchestra: Miss Cameron Jimenez!"

Peter and Elias had to shove Cameron on both shoulders before she understood the meaning of what Mr. Smith had just said. They had chosen her. The audience had voted for her. It was incredible.

She walked onstage into the lights, and applause and cheers filled the room to the high ceiling. She bowed low. The word "concertmistress" echoed in her ears. She stood up and beamed. This was the best.

Peter Smith took her arm now and ushered her off the stage. The heavy velvet curtains swept behind them, creating the privacy of backstage.

Peter and Elias were standing there in the wings. Mr. Smith went to them with his arms outstretched. "Well done, boys, well done!" he exclaimed.

"You mean it about the composition?" Elias asked.

Mr. Smith put both his hands on Elias's shoulders. "If you can write it, we'll play it," he said. "World premiere."

Elias narrowed his eyes and looked straight at Mr. Smith. Cameron could feel the intensity pouring off him. "Do you want it in the classical style?" he asked.

Mr. Smith lifted his chin and smiled slightly. "I want it to have style," he said. "I want it to move me. But I would be disappointed if it was something I had heard before."

Elias grinned. "Well, it won't be," he promised.

"And be sure to write a violin solo," Peter said, with a challenging look at Cameron.

"Yup," Cameron said. "Because I've promised to break my wrist for the concert."

Mr. Smith looked at each of them in turn. He, the conductor who freely corrected but rarely praised, smiled at them. The look in his eyes was one of welcome. He was seeing them now, not as children, but as musicians, and he was proud of what he saw.

"I think," he said carefully, "you'd better make the solo for oboe."

Dian Curtis Regan

TANGLED NOTES IN WATERMELON

After my grandmother died, we found boxes of guitar picks in her room. In drawers and on closet shelves. All colors. Most with logos, like: Fender, or bands: The Grateful Dead, or vacation destinations: Branson!

The oddness of it—especially the thought of my grandmother at a Grateful Dead concert—made me laugh, even though I'd been crying at her graveside in the brisk October gusts only an hour before.

Heart attack. No warning. I keep wandering in and out of her room, hoping I'll find her there. Seems cruel to still catch whiffs of the Avon perfume she used to over-spritz.

Propped against her dresser mirror is my school picture. On the back, she'd scribbled "Cora 16 yrs." Next to the photo is a ring dish shaped like a musical note. I gave it to her for her sixty-sixth birthday two weeks ago.

Eight thin rings fill the dish. Gran used to switch them, one by one, from her left hand to her right to keep track of her eight daily glasses of water. They were made of copper to ease the arthritis that flared up whenever she played her music.

Seeing the rings next to her sturdy Tupperware water tumbler zings my heart. I wish Mom had left them on Gran's fingers when they took her to the funeral home.

I'm an only child. Was as close to my grandmother as two keys on a piano. I'm named after her: Cora Kathleen. My father left when I was three, so Mom took back her maiden name, Cabalo, and moved us in with Gran, where we've lived ever since.

Another reason my grandmother and I were close is because I inherited something unusual from her: I see colors and shapes when I listen to music.

▪▪▪▪

Retreating to my room, I settle onto the bed, still wearing the navy jumper Mom made me wear to the funeral. I plug earphones into my CD player and let Beyoncé kick off my color music extravaganza. Her mellow voice fills the room with lavender cotton candy. Doesn't matter whether I close my eyes or leave them open. The show begins as soon as notes waltz into my ears.

Jazz is the prettiest. Its funky beat slides up and

down the scale from lipstick pink to fuchsia. When I crank up the volume, it leaps to screaming violet.

Rock and roll is orange and jittery. Not solid orange, but layers of yellows, reds, and an impossibly brilliant rust. For some reason, these jumpy colors make me nervous. Soul music is dark—slate gray, tinged with a somber dusty rose. I find soul colors depressing.

The short explanation of my "condition" is a cross-wiring of sensory areas in the brain. It's called synesthesia. Everyone who has it experiences it differently, but when two or more senses attack you all at once, it can be very distracting.

I was seven years old when my mother discovered I was like Gran. Mom and I were singing along with songs on my Barney tape recorder when I asked why the notes were hopping around the room like Little Bo Peep's sheep—turning from pale blue, like Bo's dress, to yellow, like her hair.

Even now, I remember how quiet Mom became. She clicked off the music and scooped me up, holding me for a long time. Then she took me down the hall to tell Gran.

My grandmother's reaction was the opposite of Mom's. I could tell by her slow smile that she was pleased. "Don't let anyone say you're crazy," she warned. "Normal people do not know what they're missing." (I remember this only because of the times my mom has repeated it.)

That night, Gran and I settled onto the sofa to watch a movie called *Fantasia*. I couldn't believe it.

Dancing on the TV screen were notes! Just like I saw in real life. Only the colors were all wrong. Didn't everyone see harp music as plum waterfalls splashing upon rainbow rocks?

"Cora!"

Mom is standing in the doorway, hollering my name so I can hear her above the music. I yank off the headphones to see what she wants.

"You okay?" she asks. I can tell she's been crying.

I hold out my arms. Mom sinks onto the bed for a hug. She's changed into sweats and is probably wondering why I haven't ditched the jumper and gone back to my "uniform": faded low-riders with clunky clogs and a skinny tee.

"How's pizza sound?" she asks, smoothing my hair. "I'm not up for going out tonight—or cooking. We can have a pizza delivered and eat here."

"Fine. No meat, please. Veggies."

Standing, Mom frowns at the ceiling the way she does when pretending to talk to God. "Where did I go wrong? My child asks for vegetables."

I want to laugh, but I'm still thinking about the funeral, which makes it hard to crack a smile. "Mom?" I ask. "Who was that guy?"

"What guy?"

"At the church. The one about my age. He came late and sat in the back. At the grave site, he stood by the pines along the fence."

"I didn't notice him. Maybe he was one of Gran's music students."

Logical answer.

My grandmother had a degree in music from Juilliard. She could play any instrument—piano, guitar, lute, violin, saxophone. She once played flute in a symphony orchestra, but had to leave—not because she wasn't good enough, but because she kept asking other musicians questions like, *How does Mozart's* Linzer *Symphony in C Major taste to you? Are the notes you see floating from the oboe misty green? Do you like the way they collide with the black rectangles exploding from the cymbals?*

Once she told the conductor how the rhythm of the violas swirled around her in shades of periwinkle, making her feel amorous. (Yes, "amorous." That was the exact word she used. Not a word you'd find in *my* vocabulary.)

Mom didn't like Gran sharing all this with me. My mother did not have the "Cabalo curse," as she called our strange ability, nor did she understand it. The whole time she was growing up, people whispered about Gran having mental problems. Mom told me how mortified she'd felt, even though she'd known the rumors were not true.

▪▪▪▪

The conductor of the symphony finally asked Gran to leave. He took her out to dinner to fire her. Imagine that. An organist was playing show tunes at the restaurant, and even though the music was lively and upbeat, Gran told me the entire room turned a scratchy charcoal gray and made her cry.

After that, Gran taught music at a private

school. For a time it was fine. Then she began to ask students what certain notes smelled like to them. And if they saw colors *after* they hit the keys, strummed the strings, or tapped the drums. Or if they saw colors *first,* then heard the music.

Students loved her, but in their enthusiasm they said too much to their parents, who called the principal with questions about this strange new teacher—who didn't last very long.

Next she taught at international schools in Nigeria, Japan, Brazil, and the Philippines. It was a way to see the world and hear other cultures' music, she told me. And she learned not to say too much about the Cabalo curse.

When she returned to the States, she brought back a daughter, the result of a brief marriage to a Filipino musician—brief because he could not accept her odd quirk.

Gran raised my mom (and then me) in her tiny apartment, offering private music lessons to pay the bills. She did this for the rest of her life, taking in students while Mom was at work and I was at school.

▪▪▪▪

"Can you get the door?" Mom hollers from the kitchen.

I'm in the midst of changing into jeans and a purple tee. I yank the shirt over my head and run barefoot to the living room. Grabbing the pizza money off the piano, I open the door.

Standing on the porch is not the pizza guy.

It's the guy from Gran's funeral.

"May I come in?" he asks.

All the warnings about letting strangers into one's house slide out of my memory because of the look on his face. His eyes are red and puffy. He's been crying. And he's giving me a pleading look, like if I don't let him in, his world will end.

I let him in.

He walks to my grandmother's piano and sits down as if he's done this many times before. He begins to play soft and slow.

I don't know the tune, yet the melody pinches my heart with so much emotion, it seems as if he's making up a song about this depressing day.

My color music show begins. I see arrows, a dark shade of teal, flying off the piano keys. I doubt anyone else could see them. Maybe Gran. The arrows swirl *a tempo* with the music, slow-flying around the lamp next to the piano. I am transfixed.

"Did you remember to tip him?" my mother calls.

For an instant, I have no idea what she's talking about. Then the doorbell rings again.

I'm still clutching the pizza money. Reluctantly, I abandon the stranger playing his haunting funeral dirge and open the door to the real pizza guy, who happens to be a girl.

I take the box and hand her extra money. A generous tip. I don't know why I feel like doing this. Maybe it's because of the way she's cocking her head toward the music, or perhaps it's the melancholy smile spreading across her face as if the melody is triggering sad but pleasant memories.

Closing the door, I stand there barefoot with the pizza box, feeling stupid, not sure what to do. The music stops, and the guy looks up at me. His eyes are the same dark teal as the arrows. They pierce my heart.

"Would you like to have dinner with us?" I ask, shocked by my own boldness.

He nods. Rising from the piano bench, he takes the pizza from my grip as if he wants to lighten my burden on this awful day.

Between the teal melody and his gentle gesture, I fall in love.

We go into the kitchen. He sets the pizza on the table.

"Oh," my mother says as she clunks ice into two glass mugs. "I thought you paid him, Cora."

"This is not the pizza guy," I tell her. "This is, um, a friend. I've invited him to stay for dinner."

"Oh," my mother says. "Oh."

She reaches for a third mug and drops ice into it. Just like that.

▪ ▪ ▪ ▪

I put another plate and napkin on the table and begin to sweat. Any second my mom is going to pull me aside to ask why I would invite a stranger to dinner on the day of her mother's funeral. And I don't even know his name.

"Thank you," the guy says as she offers him salad. "I'm Jesse Caldwell. I go to school with Cora."

I stare at him, wondering how he knows my name. Did Mom say it when we walked into the kitchen? Or is this guy a con artist? I don't remember him from school.

Did I just let a robber into our apartment? Before I can panic, Jesse gives me an apologetic look, as if he knows he's put me in an uncomfortable situation. He winks, and I know it's a secret promise to help end the awkwardness by charming my mother. I relax. No one who shows up at the door in tears, plays piano like an angel, then winks at me like we're old friends could possibly be a criminal.

In this alternate universe I've suddenly stumbled into, we small-talk our way through dinner, distracting Mom by discussing school stuff. I don't actually *say* these school experiences are ones Jesse and I have shared at Mulling High, yet she doesn't question it.

Mom apologizes for not having dessert to offer. She shoos us into the living room after the table is cleared. I am still existing in my state of nonreality, but at least I can stop watching what I say in front of Mom.

▪▪▪▪

"Can we go for a walk?" Jesse asks.

I put on shoes, grab a jacket, and tell Mom. Then I slip her cell phone into my pocket—just in case a 911 call becomes necessary.

But I have nothing to worry about. Jesse stays silent all the way down the block to the park. A harvest moon, fat and yellow, lights our way. I gaze at it, willing the moon goddess to give me enough nerve to ask Jesse what's going on.

We circle a playground, then sit in the dugout of a ball field. The lights are on, but no one is on the diamond.

"You must have been a student of my grandmother's," I venture.

"Yes, I was," he says. "But she was more than a teacher to me."

"What do you mean?"

He glances my way, then bows his head and kicks at a chain-link fence. "When I tell people, they think I'm crazy. But not your grandmother. She knew exactly what I was talking about."

Ahhh. And so now do I. "You're a synesthete," I say.

His head jerks up and he stares at me. "Well, of course you'd know about it, because of your grandmother." He pauses while a group of screaming kids dash across the field. "Do you believe it's true? Or did you think she was crazy?"

"I believe it's true," I assure him. "Because I have it, too."

The gasp, the surprise in his eyes, the pleasure my confession brings him. I want to know this guy. I want to find out if I hear music when he kisses me.

"Do you really go to Mulling?" I ask, suppressing my romantic urge and hoping he can't read minds as well.

"Yes, I'm a senior. I don't remember seeing you there, either, but I take classes only in the morning, then study—or *used* to study—with Mrs. Cabalo in the afternoons while you were at school. I saw your picture on the wall and recognized you at the funeral."

His voice wavers. "I can't believe she's . . ."

"Neither can I." The notes from his song play through my head. I will always hear them when I think of the death of my grandmother.

Jesse shifts toward me on the bench. "Tell me about your gift," he begins. "What do you see and hear and taste and smell when you listen to music? I want to know there's someone else who experiences the same things I do. Someone besides your grandmother."

"I'm not as talented as you two." I hope he appreciates the fact I'm referring to his ability as a *talent* and not a curse. "I see shapes and colors. That's all."

"Do the notes ever tangle on you?"

At first I don't know what he means, but then it hits me. I'd asked Gran once about the tangly images I see when a musician slides a finger up and down piano keys or guitar strings. She told me the musical term: *glissando*.

"Hey, I know what you're talking about," I say, pleased to understand something I formerly took for granted. "When the notes tangle, they become watermelon-colored."

"I see them as butterscotch."

"No kidding?"

"In fact," he adds, "watermelon is what I see and taste when I hear the name Cora."

I'm not quite sure how to take this. "So, um, do you *like* watermelon?"

He laughs. "Oh, yes. If your name made me taste, say, *broiled liver,* we might have a problem." He nudges me to show he's teasing. "So what does the name Jesse do for you?"

I want to tell him it makes my heart crescendo, but hormonal reactions have nothing to do with synesthesia. "I don't see or taste or smell or hear anything," I admit.

Disappointment tilts his head.

Oh, great, I've hurt his feelings. "I didn't mean it in a bad way," I assure him. "It just happens differently for me."

"You mean, names or numbers don't have taste or gender?"

"Gender?" I know that some people assign colors or taste to letters, or even months and days, but *gender*?

"Yeah," he says. "Red is female. Twenty-something. Yellow is a little girl. Brown is young and male. I'm not sure what gray is, but green is an older man."

This is news to me. "Whatever you say," I tell him.

"I say that I'm very happy to find someone else I can talk to about synesthesia. When I got the news that your grandmother died, I thought I'd have to stifle this for the rest of my life. Censor myself every time I start to say the wrong thing—like how the word "Chicago" tastes like melted cheese, and every time I hear it, I want to eat a grilled Swiss sandwich."

I start to laugh but see that he's being serious. "Have you ever been there?"

"To Chicago? No. Don't think I could stand tasting cheese for days on end."

I am loving this ease of teasing with each other, but guilt kicks in and I think of my mom, home alone on the night she's buried her mother. "I should get back."

"Sure," he says, standing and leading me out of the dugout. The temperature has dropped so much, even the moon looks cold. I zip my jacket and yank up the hood.

"What instruments do you play?" he asks as we find the path that leads to the edge of the park.

"None."

He looks at me as if I've told him I don't have ears. "You lived with your grandmother and never took lessons from her?"

"She *tried* to teach me, but how could I pay attention when melodies were dancing all over the room, changing colors? She finally gave up."

He shakes his head like he knows exactly what I'm talking about. "It takes focus to learn the notes and block out the distraction. I remember how hard the first lessons were—but I really wanted to learn."

"I don't think we perceive things the same

way," I say. "I mean, I know country music is always sharp-angled, and comes to me in shades of peach, lime, and banana yellow. But I don't know how it tastes or how the texture feels, like you do."

He nods as if he's a bit sorry for me, which starts me wondering if I *am* missing something by not having a more "severe" case of synesthesia.

"But now that Gran is gone, you can talk to *me* about it," I tell him.

"Thank you, Cora."

He takes my hand as we walk down the side-walk. I feel as if my grandmother has given me a gift from the grave. *Look, Gran! Your boy prodigy and namesake granddaughter, hand in hand, sharing the Cabalo curse.*

I'll bet she's smiling down on us right now, delighting in the fact that I'm feeling "amorous" toward her prize student. (Maybe she gave me that word because she knew I'd be needing it soon. . . .)

"So, what does *your* name make you think of?" I can't help but ask.

"Jesse? It's actually my middle name. I prefer it over my first, Theodore. That word grates against me like sandpaper, so I dropped it. I like the taste and color of Jesse. I see shades of soft brown, sort of like milk chocolate."

"And brown is male."

"Yes, brown is male," he repeats, looking pleased that I remembered. "Hey, after all this talk of food, why don't we pick up dessert and take it back for your mother?"

"Something chocolate?" I ask.

"Or watermelon." He squeezes my hand. "I'm starting to become a *huge* fan of watermelon."

I feel myself blush, and don't know what to say. All I can think about is what kind of color music show we will see and hear together.

Especially when he kisses me.

Jude Mandell
BALLAD OF A PRODIGY

Stanza I

My mother laughs,
telling interviewers
that when I was little,
I'd come home from school
either crying or singing,
broadcasting my mood
in tones
audible
two blocks away.
It didn't take much to raise my voice in sobs:
the sight of sightless *lapins*
hanging in the butcher-shop window,
stripped of their long ears and soft gray fur,
the ugly yells of bare-kneed boys
from St. Francis's Academy,
shouting *"Chicken-soup kike!"*

as they chased my sister and me
through the mean, cobblestoned streets
of Montreal—
the smell of blood on Sherre's
bruised knuckles, battle stains
she won fist-fighting those rowdy,
pea-soup-eating French hooligans,
in hopes of distracting them
from flinging mud and rocks
at me,
her crybaby sister.

Refrain

Though music sings inside of me,
I wonder if your plans for me
are who and what I really am,
and who and what I'm meant to be.

Stanza II

Those early days,
the days before
they discovered I was
A VOICE,
singing was as natural as breathing.
I'd raise notes in my throat
and burst out,
spontaneous,
heedless of eavesdroppers,
the music in me
spilling through the seams
of my joy.

I'd hum, or *tra-la-la,*
tuneful with delight at
the scent of mown grass
sweet in my nostrils,
the sight of funny
cloud shapes that
melted into misty rain,
the feel of a
leaf from our privet hedge
curling between my fingers,
a tiny bite of greenness,
crisp between my curious teeth.
I'd trill with anticipation,
running barefoot
up the flower-carpeted stairs,
eager for stolen moments
alone in the room I shared with
my sister, my champion.
Ah! To be solitary,
and spill out memories of the morning
in song, or watercolor shapes
splashed on rough paper.
I'd stare at Sherre's diary,
longing to be old enough to write *my* day down
on thin blue lines.
Already for me,
the words inside my head
held a melody of their own.

Refrain

Though music sings inside of me,
I wonder if your plans for me
are who and what I really am,
and who and what I'm meant to be.

Stanza III

The first time I was "discovered,"
made out to be a prodigy,
I was five years old.
It was in music class.
Such a big voice for such a little girl,
the music teacher told my mother and father,
awe in her thick-featured face.
A regular Jenny Lind. She'll sing opera someday.
My proud parents bragged about my gift,
cajoled me,
begged me,
bribed me
to sing
for the relatives,
the neighbors,
friends who stayed for dinner.
I sang on cue and was paid liberally
in sloppy kisses,
pinches that hurt my cheeks,
applause from polite hypocrites
who smelled of damp wool and mothballs
and talked through every song I sang.
Sherre, standing in the shadows,

ignored by the company,
watched hungrily,
never noticing
how I winced at so much attention.
With the swiftness of a grace note
I would have traded in the limelight
she craved
for the *andante* tempo of my old
anonymity.
A poem swam inside my head
about how sad it felt to watch her face,
about how scared I was
the singing would become so big
that *I* would disappear.
Someday, I thought, I'll write that poem down.

Refrain

Though music sings inside of me,
I wonder if your plans for me
are who and what I really am,
and who and what I'm meant to be.

Stanza IV

My mom, who counted every penny
in the lean days when every penny counted,
stretched our meager budget to ensure
I got the music lessons
recommended—
voice lessons once I reached puberty,
piano right away.

She bought an old Knabe upright
and hired four panting movers
to push and pull it
into our musty basement.
Mr. Berg, my teacher, upright as the Knabe,
saw me twice a week.
I strained and stretched
my stubby fingers to reach those octaves.
His teeth, chipped and yellowed
like old piano keys,
never showed a smile.
Tight-lipped and scowling, he
rapped my knuckles to encourage me.
I hadn't known before
that music could bring pain.
Afterward, my small hands hurt so much, I cried.

He never noticed tears, just kept on counting beats.
Rhythm drove him, and ambition,
not a caring for the prodigies
whom he'd made famous.
I wrote about him in my diary for years,
trying to decide what lay inside that barrel chest.
No human heart, I thought. Instead,
a beating metronome, metallic, merciless.
My sister Sherre tapped keys, too,
typing on an old Underwood typewriter
my parents bought her, secondhand.
The teachers had been up to their old tricks again,
deciding Sherre's wheel of fortune stopped at
Secretary.
The two of us were typecast

in the cement
of good intentions,
each following the plan laid out for us,
stereotyped before we knew what we were all about.

Refrain

Though music sings inside of me,
I wonder if your plans for me
are who and what I really am,
and who and what I'm meant to be.

Stanza V

Sometimes I stole time from practicing
to roller-skate or hopscotch
with the neighbors' kids.
I worried I might lose these friends
unless I sometimes came outside to play.
Mom said she understood.
I needed time to be a child, too.
But if I failed to quickly memorize
the aria for my recital,
assigned to me by Mr. Satikoff,
my wire-haired voice teacher with the bad breath,
I couldn't meet Mom's stern, accusing gaze
or Dad's lost look of disappointment
without a clutch of fear.
I wanted Dad to realize his dream—
the vision that his youngest child
would be an opera star someday
gave him hope of a stature

he hadn't reached in inches,
or education.
Dad never realized
his kindnesses to us and others
made him, in our eyes,
a bigger man than anybody knew.
Mom scrimped and saved
to give me opportunities she never had.
She rolled the money Dad earned
thin as pie crust, stretching it transparent,
all to help my talent grow.
I owed them both.
I owed my sister, too.
I wrote more poems in my diary about her.
How I wished with all my heart
we had enough
to buy the colored bobby socks she begged for
in every shade,
all the rage in Philadelphia,
where we had moved
when Dad lost another job.
Each time my sister wailed about those socks,
Mom smoothed her forehead with cool palms:
Be patient, Dear. If Dad can't find work, maybe I can.
But for now, your sister's music lessons must come first.

Refrain

Though music sings inside of me,
I wonder if your plans for me
are who and what I really am,
and who and what I'm meant to be.

Stanza VI

By age eleven I was on TV,
The Children's Hour, a weekly show,
famous as a stepping stone to Stardom—
Broadway maybe, or Hollywood.
Every Tuesday night, and all day Saturday,
my family put their lives on hold for me,
waiting while I rehearsed my lines and songs
with the other prodigies.
Saturday we blocked the scenes in Studio C,
cavernous, dim, with cold cement floors.
In there, my strong voice evaporated,
sucked up by microphones
and the stratospheric height
of soundproofed ceilings.
By 11:30 A.M. Sunday,
the plush theater seats in Studio A
were filled with our faithful fans.
My parents brought Sherre with us all three days,
still in plain white bobby socks,
sullen, resentful,
her social life disrupted
by me, the Prima Donna,
who, it seemed, got everything she wanted.
While I sweated under the hot lights,
mouth dry with wondering if I would ever
be good enough to please our finicky director
and make my parents proud,
Sherre steamed, fueled by hormone power,
with a hot sensuality
that made cameramen stare

and my parents worry.
They brought along her portable Underwood
and typing books
to keep her out of trouble. She left them idle,
strolling off to flirt with Rod, our Teen Star,
whose main claim to fame
was resembling James Dean.
Between my scenes, the Underwood tugged
like an undertow.
Words were music too, the poems I wrote
a way of learning who I could become.
And how my right hand tired,
filling all those diaries!
I memorized the letter keys in fifteen minutes.
The finger strokes took ten.
Child's play compared to Mozart.

Refrain

My words and music sing to me
of choices that were made for me.
I know the who I am right now,
and who and what I'd like to be.

Stanza VII

I typed my first set of lyrics on that old Underwood,
reworked from poems in my diaries.
The music that I set them to
sprang from somewhere
underneath my breastbone,
a raw place
that has yet to heal.

My first album topped the charts.
I called it *Sherre: Songs My Sister Never Sang,*
all about how the two of us
grew up together
and the joy and pain of
loving one another.
It's not opera.
Rock with a few blues riffs mixed in.
But still, Dad's walkin' taller now,
and Mom is pleased I've found my *métier.*
I thought Sherre never would
forgive me
using her name like that.
It took a whole set of hopelessly outdated
bobby socks
in rainbow colors
to get her to start laughing with me again.
She wore the hot-pink ones
under her robe at high school graduation.
Our private joke.
She's vowed to wear the rest,
if she can ever get up enough nerve
to go to fashion school.
I'm counting on it.

My second album got released today.
Billboard magazine went wild,
called me:
"A Teen Phenom!
A Prodigy."
It gave us all a laugh.

Refrain

My words and music set me free
to balance my own harmony,
the who and what I am right now,
the who and what I choose to be.

Jennifer Armstrong
THE SONG OF STONES RIVER

By July of 1862 the War Between the States had already torn fifteen months off the calendar. Our boys had fought bloodily in the battlefields of Virginia and on the other side of the Appalachians, too, in Tennessee, Kentucky, and Missouri. With all the cards against them—fewer men, fewer guns, fewer supplies of all kinds—the rebel army of the Confederacy had won battle after battle. Our powerful army of the United States was getting kicked all over the map. The Rebs were beating us Yankees.

Over in Murfreesboro, Tennessee, Federal troops under Major General Buell were looking to hold control of the railroad lines so the supply trains could come through from Kentucky with food for men, horses, and mules. Like a summer storm, Confederate cavalry crashed down upon them, overwhelmed the garrison, and forced a surrender. The way was now clear for the Rebels to invade northward.

And northward they ran, into Kentucky, hastening upward toward Ohio like a burning fuse, even as the sun beat down from a cloudless sky and squeezed every particle of moisture from the landscape. My brother was in a Union regiment at Green River Bridge in September when the advancing Confederate army under General Braxton Bragg broke upon them and forced another surrender. The rebel cavalry watered their dry horses at the river's edge while the defeated boys of the Union garrison were made prisoners of war, my brother among them.

Now more divisions of the Union army under Major General Rosencrans, and me and my drum with them, had to trudge south along the rail lines to beat back the Confederate invasion of Kentucky. By early October, the drought had burned the ground coal-hard, and we were worn to a thread before we'd even met the Rebels. Me beating cadence on my drum was the only beating going on at that warm time. From north and from south, footsore soldiers marched under a blistering sun, and we shook the last drops of water from our canteens; the bugler was too dry to blow his horn. We came upon a creek in Perryville, with a unit of Arkansas soldiers refreshing themselves in the shade, and this lit off a huge battle that ended with victory for us at last. By nightfall the scorched Confederates were beating a retreat back toward the Cumberland Gap, back into Tennessee. The summer campaign had beaten us all as dry and thin as leather straps, and them weary Confederate troops were looking forward to settling in for their winter camp and singing restful songs.

But we was on our way to the Cumberland Gap, too. Throughout the fall, I drummed us after the retreating Rebels, southward across the mountains into east Tennessee, and then dogged them west on the road to Nashville. Our pickets skirmished with theirs, kicking up the dust in the dry lanes as the leaves began to fall. Autumn's crops lay forgotten in the fields—pumpkins and apples abuzz with yellow jackets while the people in the countryside tried to keep out of the way of us bluecoats. Woodpeckers drummed their warning through deep thickets, and mourning doves sang their melancholy laments as we passed by. When late December's darkness closed in around us, we and the Confederates both were camped outside Murfreesboro, Tennessee, in the rocky cedar glades along the banks of the narrow Stones River.

There would be another battle. Not a man among us doubted it, though we in the ranks was too far below the officers to be informed to the level of certainty. Even though the summer and fall had been one long weary march broken up with bitter fighting, there would be no rest for us. Even though it was Christmas, there would be no rest for us. In our camp, men wrote letters to their wives and mothers as they crouched near the cook-fires. And I had no misgivings but that General Bragg's boys were doing the same over where they lay, in their bivouacs on the cold limestone. In the rope corrals, the bony mules who pulled our baggage wagons brayed their complaints into the darkness, and it seemed to me that I could let out just as desolate a cry without much effort. In the fields beyond the woods, a cold wind blew through the last ragged tatters of cotton stuck on the dry and trembling stems. Christmas came, and with it came heartache and lonesomeness. The chill breeze brought tears to my eyes. Or maybe it was thoughts of home—my ma, my little sisters. I'd been so proud to show off my drum and rattle the sticks for them. I did not know music could lead me to such a place.

Why am I here? I wondered as I thought of my home, my dog, my companions in tag and school sums. What is this war for? From each encampment, the spark and flash of campfires were visible: tomorrow the spark and flash would be artillery blasts and musket fire, and winter sunlight would glitter on bayonets. From each encampment, the low murmur of voices mingled with the mutter of water over stones; tomorrow the stones would resound with the din and discord of shots and screams, and I would play the cadence that drove men forward into death.

To raise our spirits, the regimental band began to play. Our fellows let loose with "Yankee Doodle," and it rang like metal in the frosty air. I blew on my fingers to warm them before I could get a proper grasp on the drumsticks.

Then we heard a band on the rebel side strike up "Dixie," vying to drown us out.

Our boys hollered to our band to play "The Star-Spangled Banner," and in between the bars our ears caught the strains of "Bonnie Blue Flag."

Back and forth we fought with songs, firing ourselves into the kind of hot excitement a man needs to carry him into deadly battle. The fellows grabbed their muskets by the hand, as if they was their sweethearts at a square dance, and breathed hard and remembered the fights they'd already seen and the lead they'd already let fly.

But then, in a lull, one of the bands—and I can't say which side it come from—began a quieter tune, and all around me the fellows felt their hearts catch in their throats. I lowered my drum. The words of the familiar song came to our lips, where moments before we had been thirsty for battle cries.

"'Mid pleasures and palaces though I may roam,
Be it ever so humble, there's no place like home!"

The tender words rose into the air with the sparks of the campfires on both sides, and our hearts were soothed and gentled. *"Home!"* we sang, all of us, Yankee and Rebel alike. *"Home! Sweet, sweet home! There's no place like home!"* If there is a sweeter tune, it has not been sung for living ears.

When the sun arose, the dread war would start anew, but for that moment in Tennessee we were all just Americans, singing in harmony, and our country was whole again.

Gail Giles

THE GYPSY'S VIOLIN

When I draw my bow along the violin's strings, birds burst into flight. They soar and dip and take to the blue sky, but their wings cast shadows on my face.

Those shadows are dark, not unlike these words on this paper. In writing these words, words of my song and my life, I am one of the Rom no longer.

I am Rupa. I was born of the Rom—Gypsies to the rest of the world. Until I was twelve, my life was *jallin' a drom,* or traveling the road in the brightly colored caravans. It was a world I loved, but it was a world hated by others. And it was a world that changed forever when I found the Gadje boy on the bank of the river.

▪▪▪▪

The boy bent over the creek. The oak trees, their leaves thick, made dark shadows, and as he dipped his hands into the clear water, the wind stirred the leaves. They shivered and parted as shafts of sunlight slanted through the leaf gaps. Just as drops of water fell from the Gadjo's fingers, the sunbeams kissed the droplets, turning them into dancing jewels of white light, with ghosts of color flashing at the edges. Green, yellow, blue, pink, and purple winked and shimmered from the boy's fingertips.

The Rom live in a world cloaked by the mists of mystery. We believe in signs and omens. And a sign sent by nature—one whispered by trees, carried by wind, sung by water, or written by the sun—is dangerous to ignore.

I stood still, shocked into amazement. This boy had the blessing of the elements. He held powerful magic in his hands. According to the Rom, luck traveled with him, and to walk away would be thinking myself stronger than the gods.

I watched, myself and the boy both in shadow, and then his hands dipped again and caught the water. He brought it to his mouth and shook his hands. The sun stabbed out of the trees again, and diamonds flew from his fingers.

The wind stirred the leaves as the boy slurped from his cupped hands again, and he was washed with light. He sat back on his haunches. He was young, with dark, wild hair, and he was dirty.

Later, when the trouble came, I was told that I brought the Devil into our camp. But I don't know, even now, the difference between good and evil. I think they might be found in the same thought, body, or place at different times.

"You should put your head in now and wash your face," I said. The elements may have ordained him a blessed one, but that did not stop my sassy tongue. He spun as he scrambled to his feet.

He looked eleven or twelve. I peered at him as I stood with one hip cocked out. I held my wooden bucket with one hand; the other shaded my eyes from the sunbeams that now danced on the singing water.

The breeze stirred his hair, and he rubbed his mouth with the back of his hand. Fear marched across his face.

"Don't look so frightened. I thought *you* were a ghost, but . . ." I pulled a crust from my pocket. "Look, I've got my bread."

His forehead creased in puzzlement. Ah, what could I expect from a Gadje boy? "Bread," I explained. "It protects me from witches, ghosts, or bad luck." I put the bread back into my pocket. "So you must be harmless." I smiled and swung my bucket, making my skirts sway. "Even if you do smell like a chicken yard."

He stood—sun, shadow, and dirt dappling his shocked face. I wondered for a moment if his mouth held no tongue, or his head no brain.

"You're dressed in a rainbow," he finally said.

I smiled again. Yellow and red ribbons tried to tame my curls, and my skirt swirled long and full of color: red, yellow, green, and blue. Gold loops dangled from my ears and copper bracelets danced on my arms. My feet were bare and dusty, and my toes twitched and grabbed at the sparse spears of grass.

"You need to wash your clothes and your body," I said. "But you have to go downstream to do that."

The Gadje boy had yet to move. He seemed to have rooted to the earth, like the dark trunks of the trees all around us.

I skipped past him and swung my bucket down into the creek, then back in one motion that disturbed the song of the water as little as possible. The sun skipped on the rivulets and, as I stood there, the brightness of the creek seemed to divide me from the boy as he waited in the dimness of the forest.

I stayed, balanced on a flat stone, and faced his shadow. "The river is for drinking." I pointed. "Farther down is for washing dishes and for baths. Down still more is water for the horses and the bear."

"Bear?" His question drifted to me on the breeze.

I stepped off the stone and onto the bank, then took two steps so that we both stood in the shade. "The dancing bear."

The questions rode his face, but he did not ask them.

I sighed. "Farthest downstream is for washing clothes."

The Gadje boy finally moved. He sat down on a tuft of grass and leaned back against the trunk of the tree. His shoulders slumped in his ragged clothes and I could see that he was tired, the kind of tired that a nap won't cure.

"Why do you have all these rules? Why don't you just wash everything in the same place?"

I gave him a long stare, hard enough to show him that he had said something wrong. "You Gadje. You call the Rom dirty and then say something like that." I twitched my skirt again and stamped my foot, just a small stamp on the ground. I began to stroll away.

"What's the Rom?"

I stopped and turned to look back. Who was this boy, that he could be so stupid?

"Rom," I said. "The Gadje call us Gypsies."

He stood and sidled behind the tree.

"What's wrong with you?" I asked.

"I've heard that Gypsies are evil. They cast spells and steal things. I even heard that they kidnap babies."

The sun sank lower, and an orange haze filtered through the darkening shadows. The haze was the color of my anger. "You're not a baby, are you?" I flung the question at him like a stone. "And you're too skinny for anyone to want to kidnap."

The Gadje boy rubbed his eyes, and the orange haze began to pale as purple took its place over the creek. "The Nazis don't think so."

The word made my breath turn solid in my lungs. The trees seemed to turn into men with reaching arms and clutching fingers.

"You are not of the Rom, so that's not why the Nazis want you. So you must be . . ."

"Jew," he said.

"The Nazis are Gadje, but you're afraid of the Gypsies? The Nazis hate the Rom as much as they hate the Jew."

He nodded, solemn. His thoughts were as clear to me as if he had shouted them.

"Gadje," I said, my voice frosted with scorn.

"What's a Gadje?" he asked.

No wonder this boy was dirty and lost. He must have been dropped on his head and addled. I opened my mouth to answer this stupid boy when a voice sneaked over my shoulder.

"Gadje is anyone that's not Gypsy."

Grandmother stood behind me. "You were away so long, Rupa. I came to see if you had found some mischief." She swept the Gadje boy with her eyes. "Maybe it found you."

Grandmother moved closer to the boy. She stiffened and stepped back. She made a quick sign with two fingers of her right hand, then rubbed her arms as if cold. She had spoken to me in Romany but switched to the Gadje tongue. "Who are you, boy, and where do you come from?"

The boy saw that Grandmother held some fear of him. It seemed to make him stronger. He spoke politely, but kept his eyes locked with Grandmother's. "I am Ben. My story is long and it is my own."

Grandmother's chin went up, but she kept her eyes fastened on the boy's. Without looking at me, she said, "Go along to camp, Rupa. Your mother needs the water for supper."

I opened my mouth to argue, but she spoke again without a glance my way. "Obey your grandmother."

I stamped away from the creek, but then slipped behind a tree and hid in its apron of shadow.

"Why do you come here," Grandmother demanded, "to the Gypsy camp?"

"I didn't know there was a camp," the boy said. "I was thirsty and heard the creek."

"Death lurks over your shoulder." Grandmother rubbed her arms again. "I don't know if Death is waiting for you or waiting to ride your shoulder into our camp."

The boy slid down and sat on the mossy earth. "I don't mean you any harm." He pushed his long hair back from his face. "You heard. I am a Jew. I've wandered the forests keeping out of sight of the Nazis. I'm lost and hungry."

"I know what it is to be hated. And hunted," Grandmother said. "And I cannot send a hungry child alone into the night. Come with me to the camp and eat. Maybe Death can be sent to trouble someone else."

I dashed for the clearing.

▪▪▪▪

A Gypsy camp is a magic circle. The wagons are as different as their owners. Some have straight sides, like the straight backs of the men who drive them. Some have arching tops, curving like the women who tend them. The *vardos* carry the joy and spirit of the Gypsy outside as they carry the stoves and beds within. Wood carvings of dragons, lions, or snakes twined with vines and leaves crawl on the sides of the wagons, and flowers mass in the corners. Angel lamps are mounted by the doors to show the carving of a horse if the owner is a horse trader, or a bear if he trains the dancing bear. Everything is painted in a riot of color. Blood red, jonquil yellow, envious green, azure, all are rimmed with gold. But there is never black. Never a hint of death.

The camp makes its own music. The ring of the hammer against copper in the *atchintan*, and the jingle of the harness as the horses are fed and curried. The crack as the ax splits the wood; the snap and hiss of the kindling in the glowing fire. The smoke swirls like the dresses of the darting, dancing women, giving every evening the feel of a festival. The men have long hair, in shoulder-tapping curls, and their white teeth shine from dusky faces as they smile. The rhythms of their voices as they call to one another, flirt with the women, or sing as they work are the heartbeat of the *campo*.

The women wear headdresses or bright kerchiefs decorated with gold coins, and heavy necklaces circle slender necks. The first song I ever played on my violin was rings and necklaces winking in the firelight and bracelets tinkling on graceful arms as the women worked.

The smoke carried the cooking smells, and they swayed and sashayed under the Gadje boy's nose.

I heard his stomach tell the story of his hunger, but his mouth did not. The Rom took what they needed. The Gadje were too proud to take or to ask. Proud makes the stomach talk but never fills it.

Then the roar. Not the Gadjo's stomach. The bear.

The boy seemed to have mice running under his skin. He jumped, his eyes searching the camp.

"It's only the bear," I told him.

He moved to the bear as if it had captured him and pulled him, with a string and a treat, into its circle. His eyes lost the fear. He looked as if he recognized someone.

The creature shuffled and lumbered in a small circle around a post pounded into the ground. It wore a heavy metal collar and a thick chain attached to the stake. The chain clanked as the bear pulled it tight, approaching the Gadjo as if they were brothers. It circled the log again and again, its shaggy head low, its eyes on the ground. Around. Around. Around.

Brown. Taller than the wheel, but not as tall as the wagon. The bear stopped its circling and stood upright. It waved thick paws in the air. Its nose was black and shiny, but its eyes were listless. The Gadje boy did not look at anything but the bear.

"I want to touch him."

His voice was a prayer. A wish. A lullaby.

"He's tame," I said. "He won't hurt you."

The boy looked past me to Grandmother. I saw her eyes grow narrow, as if seeing a spirit.

"I was like him," the Gadje boy said. "You took him from his home and you keep him prisoner. And you make him work for you. Isn't that right?"

Grandmother nodded. "His name is Coffee."

The Gadje boy drifted to the bear. His hand flowed out and touched the huge paw with quivering fingers. The bear shambled forward. The boy reached up and stroked the bear's broad nose. The bear lowered its head and the boy rubbed the top, ruffling the fur and scratching behind the ears.

"Rumpf," the bear growled low, content. *"Rumpf."*

The Gadjo stepped closer and ran his hand over the heavily muscled shoulders and down the bear's front legs. He pushed his face into the bear's neck and nuzzled the coarse fur, breathing in the musky scent.

"Rumpf."

"I know," the Gadjo whispered. "Your name isn't Coffee at all, is it?"

"Rumpf."

The Gadjo's laugh was full and ripe, dripping like a plump peach. Listening to it was like being caught in a summer rain.

"I think you're trying to teach me something." The boy leaned to the bear and spoke close to its ear. "Your name is Rumpf, isn't it?"

The boy looked pleased. The bear roared and waved its paws, then sat down. *"Rumpf."*

The Gadjo laughed again. I wanted to play his laugh on my violin.

But Grandmother watched with her funeral face. She spoke no words, but she flicked her fingers, warding off the Devil. Her brow pushed into its worry place and her lips grew tight. "Come," she said. "Dinner waits."

The Gadjo looked at us, awakened from his bear dream. "Yes," he said. He bent down and rubbed the bear's ears. "I'll be back soon," he said.

"Rumpf."

Grandmother led and I trailed behind, past the gossiping women and the children who danced, and chased, and squealed. We came to our green wagon with yellow painted flowers that twined around the small shuttered windows. My father, my mother, and my two annoying brothers were gathered around our cooking fire. I settled, cross-legged, on the ground with them.

"Daughter," Grandmother said. "I bring a Gadje boy to share our dinner."

My mother gazed up at the old woman with questions in her dark eyes. They did not speak, but after a moment Mother nodded at Grandmother as if her questions had been answered.

"I'll get you a plate," she told the boy. "There was luck today, and Pulinka caught a hedgehog."

"Baked hedgehog," I said. "It seems like a feast day."

"Did you save the feet?" Grandmother asked.

Mother gestured toward the wagon. "Of course,"

she said. Her smile was as bright as the bracelets on her arm. "Nothing sends a toothache away as well as a hedgehog foot."

I could see the contest in the Gadje boy's face. Jewish boys must not be fond of hedgehog. But hunger won, and he picked up the meat and bit. When the rich juices flowed into his mouth, he closed his eyes and chewed rapidly, greedily, licking his fingers when he finished.

I handed him a tin mug. "Coffee." We smiled at our joke.

He took the mug in both hands. "Thank you."

"He has made friends with the bear," I said.

Pulinka, my father, cocked his head, much as the bear had done. "That bear likes no one."

"He's just sad," the Gadje boy said.

"The man who trains him might feed you if you care for the bear and exercise him," I said. "He wanted me to do it."

"Can I sleep with him, too?"

I laughed. My laugh is like the caw of a crow. There is no music inside. No summer rain. Just a squawk, with a ruffling of feathers around it. "It sleeps under the wagon. I'm sure Terkari won't care, but . . ." I laughed again. "But you might ask the bear."

The Gadjo stood up. "Thank you for the dinner," he said. "I have never eaten hedgehog before, and it was very good." He nodded to Grandmother. "You've been very kind to me." He looked at me. "I will go ask if I can sleep with the bear now." He moved away.

"Terkari is playing music with the men over there." My father pointed in a different direction.

The Gadje boy shrugged and continued in the direction he had been going.

"He means to ask the bear," I said.

▪ ▪ ▪ ▪

I climbed into the wagon to fetch my heart, the violin that Pulinka, my father, made for me. The graceful swan's neck led to the body that swelled and narrowed like the ebb and flow of the tides. The wood glowed like a coal on a fireplace grate. On the face, where the violin swells out to the widest point, Pulinka had inlaid a shape in a lighter shade of wood. A bear. A dancing bear.

My father's people are musicians, but my mother's people are animal trainers. My uncle is Terkari, the bear trainer. My annoying older brothers always said I was like that bad-natured bear. Always roaring. My father thought it amusing that I roared at my tall, strong brothers and didn't fear them, so he put a bear into my violin.

A Gypsy woman is not permitted to play the violin in the streets for money, any more than we are allowed to wear pants or do the horse-trading. We tell fortunes with the tarot, with the crystal ball, or by reading palms. We dance. We sell spells and potions to those who want what they do not have. We play tambourines, but not the violin.

Pulinka, my father, tried to teach my annoying older brothers to bring music from their souls through their fingers and onto the strings, but their fingers could not sing. Their fingers could not dance, and the strings cawed like my crow-laugh.

My father heard me humming songs of my own making. Songs of joy, sorrow, confusion. Songs of the brooks and the birds and the dancing of rabbits. He taught me to play the violin. He showed me how to tuck it carefully under my chin, as if I were holding an egg against my collarbone. He taught me which string sang the song of the lark, and which one the sound of the thunder. He taught me how to hold the bow and draw it across the strings as a mother caresses the hair on the head of her baby.

But the music was that of my soul dreaming.

I played that night. A moon-song of melancholy and loss, and of coming home.

▪▪▪▪

I awoke early the next morning and sat on the step of the wagon. Terkari climbed out, scratching his ribs and yawning. "Wake up, Coffee," he called. "Get up, you lazy bear." He stumbled over to the mound of brown fur under his wagon. He pulled back his foot to kick the bear and then stopped, his face a puzzle.

Curled against the bear's broad back was a skinny, dirty boy. The old man rubbed his eyes. "What?"

Grandmother appeared behind me. "A Gadje boy who is an answer to your problems, Terkari," Grandmother said.

"A Gadjo? Tekla, this is madness."

"Maybe so," Grandmother said. "But you need

someone to feed and exercise your bear. And this boy needs"—she sighed and waved her hand as if lazily waving away a fly—"someone to sing for."

That morning the women had a new chore: the cleaning of the Gadje boy. He was sent to strip off his clothes. Grandmother handed him a blanket and a lump of soap and pointed her long finger toward the creek.

"Bathe."

I saw the skin prickle along his bare shoulders and up his neck, but he nodded and dashed across the cold ground, toward the colder water.

We heard the splash and his startled yelp at nearly the same moment. More splashes and more shouts. The bear lifted his nose and ears and strained to the end of his chain, mewling and listening, worrying about his new friend-brother.

The Gadjo sped back to camp, shivering and looking like a rooster after a rainstorm. His bones told the story of long hunger. Bruises and small scars described half-healed hurt.

"Sit in the sun and warm yourself," my mother told him. "I will wash these clothes."

"Those are not clothes," I said. The sass in my mouth could not be swallowed. "Those are holes held together by dirt."

"He can wear them until a decision is made," Grandmother said.

▪▪▪▪

While Mother washed his clothes and laid them on the caravan roof to dry, I sat with the Gadjo on the steps of the wagon. The men went to the town.

They needed to look at the horses there, to check for Nazi uniforms and feel the mood of the town.

"Sing me your song, Gadjo," I said.

"If I sing, the birds will fall from the trees, the bear will go deaf, and the horses will gallop away," he said.

I made a fierce face. "That means, tell me your story. How do you come to be here, drinking from our creek and becoming a brother with our bear?"

"I will tell you, but you must promise me something." He wrapped the blanket tight around him and pushed his face close to mine. "Call me Ben, not Gadjo."

I laughed my laugh. The Gadjo pulled the blanket over his ears. "That laugh is worse than my singing," he said from inside the blanket. He poked his head back out like a river turtle stretching his neck to see what lies ahead of him.

"Fine. Ben. It's a silly Gadje name, but if you like it, I will teach my tongue to use it."

The sun was up and strong now, warming the ground, the air, and the wet boy. He relaxed against the wagon.

"My parents are in Germany. My father is well known and rich. He knew that he would not be able to leave the country. He had our butler hide me in a carter's wagon and take me to an old woman who lived in a little village. She once worked for my grandfather. She was to hide me there until arrangement could be made to get me to friends in London."

Ben's dark eyes looked as if the sun had melted

them. A tear escaped and ran down his cheek. He did not try to hide it or wipe it away. It was a badge of his loss.

"My mother and father cried when I climbed into the wagon. They held hands and said goodbye. Then I pushed down into the sacks in the cart, and more sacks were tossed over me. I left my home and everyone who ever loved me.

"There were long days in the wagon with only minutes at night to stand and walk, to eat or drink, then back among the sacks. When we reached the old woman's house, the carter gave her a sack of coins. She took it greedily but looked at me with fear. I could see she didn't want me there, but the money spoke louder.

"She had fashioned a false wall in the chicken coop. A hole hidden by a sack of feed was the entry to my new home, a space big enough for me to lie on the dirt floor under the sloping end of the shed. I could sit but not stand. I was to stay there during the day. I could come into her house only at night, to eat and to stretch."

His voice stilled. He sighed and looked at the bear chained to the pole.

"One thing saved me," Ben said. "My father put a box of books in the cart. I read them over and over again by the light that crept between the cracks in my shed. I read as the chickens clucked. I read in the cold and the dirt. I read with my nose filled with the smell of chicken droppings. I read with my stomach growling and my throat raw with thirst."

I felt a shadow hovering near me. Something

that whispered temptingly into my ear. Told me to reach for something forbidden. It felt like doom. But it felt like promise. Good and evil wrapped in the same cloak.

Then I saw Grandmother standing near us. Quiet. Worried. Her face told me not to interrupt the Gadjo's story.

"Those books," he said, "became my food and drink. My mother and father. My hope. Leaving them behind was like getting in that cart again and leaving my life to wallow in the dirt and chicken droppings."

Grandmother spoke then. "The Rom do not read or write. Our language is our own. We do not leave it lying about for others."

The Gadjo's eyes filled with surprise and something like horror. "Then how will anyone know your story when you are gone?"

"Gone? We tell our story one to the other. The stories live through our blood and our music."

"But I am alone now. My people have been taken from me and I only know of them from books," Ben said.

Grandmother harrumphed liked the big bear. "You have no books now, either."

Tears sprang to the Gadje boy's eyes. "No, the villagers found out that the woman was hiding me. They knew what the Nazis would do to them if I was found there. They drove me out with their rakes and hoes. From the edge of the forest I watched them burn my books."

Grandmother's face softened, but she turned away before the boy could see.

▪▪▪▪

The men returned from town anxious. Pulinka gathered the group around the campfire. "Nazis patrol the area. They look for Jews hiding in the villages and say they will round them up, as well as any Gypsy encampments."

My father looked hard at the Gadje boy. "Did you go into the village?"

"No," Ben said. "I know the dangers of villages. I stayed hidden in the forest."

Pulinka looked at Grandmother, who shook her head and waved at Pulinka to continue.

"We will use the rest of the day to pack up the *vardos* and be ready to leave in the morning. We must get closer to England. Wintering in England is hard, but Austria is not safe now."

Pulinka looked at eveyone. "No music tonight. Only small cooking fires. Gadjo, walk the bear down by the river all afternoon. If he does not exercise, he roars all night. It is your job to make sure he does not."

There was no merriment in the work now. No singing, no laughter. Even the bracelets lost their chime. Busy feet stirred the dust and the camp disappeared into the caravans, slung from underneath or balanced on top. Ben and I took Rumpf down to the creek.

Rumpf shambled along until he reached the forest floor; then he rolled onto his back and stretched his back legs. Ben put the bear's long chain around a tree and then we chased each other, leaping from rock to rock as Rumpf ambled behind, snuffling at the ground, looking for insects, fat grubs, or worms.

"I want you to do something for me. Something secret," I said.

Ben waited.

"Teach me to read and write."

"I thought it was forbidden."

"It is. But it is forbidden for a girl to play the violin, too. And my music needs words. My music tells stories, and I want to write them down so they can never be lost."

Ben looked at me as if I were a caged bird that belonged to someone else.

He picked up a stick and made a mark in the dirt. "That is an *R*. It's the first letter of your name."

While the bear drank from the creek and nosed behind fallen logs, I learned to write my name and Ben's name and Rumpf's name. I learned to write *cat, hat, rat, fat, sat, mat, bat, pat*. The Gadjo said I was quick and smart and should go to school. The sun was slanting low when we made our way back to camp. Just as we walked into the circle, an owl hooted a single low hoot.

The whispering stopped, as if everyone had been struck dead. The owl swooped from his branch, glided through the open circle, and then swept up past the trees and into the darkening sky. Never had there been such an omen.

A tall, gaunt woman stood and flicked the fingers of her left hand. "Go away from this place, Gadjo. Take your neighbor Death away." She stood and whisked into her wagon, and banged the wooden shutters closed.

The other Gypsies turned back to their chores but eyed Ben with suspicion.

"That's Tshaya. She is the seventh daughter of a seventh daughter," I said. "She is said to have the sight. And an owl hoot means that death is coming." I shrugged. "But owls hoot, it's what they do. And Tshaya has been wrong before. And people have died before. It has nothing to do with you."

"Will they take me along tomorrow?"

"If Grandmother tells them to, they will," I said. "She's the elder of the *kumpania*."

Ben hooked the bear to his chain and curled up against him. I walked back to our caravan humming a *cante jondo,* a deep song, one of a boy who had only one day of happiness.

▪▪▪▪

Late that night I heard the bear roar. Then shouts in German and screams. Then shots. The screaming stopped. I heard the sound of rifle butts pounding on the doors of the caravans and commands to step outside. As my mother and father pushed out onto the steps, Pulinka shoved me behind him and I felt a hand on my ankle.

The Gadje boy was under our wagon. He held his finger to his lips, motioning me to step into the shadows and crawl under the wagon with him. My father's elbow gave me permission. As I stepped to the side, my father edged over to cover me and I dropped down and under the stairs. Ben crawled backward, signaling me to follow.

We crept into the bushes, then back, farther into the forest, until we were sure we were well hidden. But we could see and hear. From the rustling and the quick glimpses of color around us, we could see that there were others who had escaped as we had.

A semicircle of Nazis pointed their guns at my people. They shouted in harsh voices that sounded like dogs barking. Other soldiers were in the caravans, pocketing things they wanted, throwing things that they didn't onto the ground, laughing as our treasures broke. I saw my violin sail through the air to land, miraculously unhurt, in the welcoming arms of a bush.

A large truck drove up, and one of the soldiers opened the back. He drove the muzzle of his rifle into Grandmother's back and pushed her. She gazed at him, unafraid, then walked into the truck. The others followed. When the doors were closed, the soldiers went from caravan to caravan and set each on fire. Then one soldier, the one with a machine gun, fired into the woods in a circle. Ben shoved me to the ground and lay on top of me as the bullets sizzled around our heads. Our heads were still down when we heard a single shot. The bear roared. Another shot and the bear was silent. I felt Ben's tears scald the back of my neck.

▪▪▪▪

The survivors of the night assembled the next morning. The Nazis did not find the horses that were kept downstream from the camp or the *vardo* of the Gypsy who cared for them. We searched the cooling caravans for anything we could save. I had my violin and nothing else.

Tshaya was one of those remaining, and we all knew that the Gadje boy could not continue the journey with us. The only thing he asked was to borrow a shovel while we packed our few belongings in the caravan.

"Why?" Tshaya demanded.

"He means to bury the bear," I told her.

▪▪▪▪

I rode on the back step of the *vardo* and played the violin as we drove away. My violin sang a song of hope for Ben the Gadje boy, a hope that he would be safe and we might find each other again.

▪▪▪▪

I left the Gypsies when I was eighteen. It was discovered that I had taught myself to read and write. I was pronounced *marimé* and cast out. I began playing my violin in public and wrote my songs down. The flags of the half notes were like the wings of birds searching over the land. I write songs of my life. My violin strings sing songs of Pulinka, my father, and of my mother and my annoying older brothers. They sing the prayer that they are alive and will hear this music and find me. My strings sing songs of the Gadje boy, Ben.

Songs of hope that he made his way to England and safety. Songs of remembrance of the Gypsy girl, Rupa. I hope that Ben will come to a concert and see the violin that Pulinka, my father, made for me. The one with the graceful swan's neck and the body that swells and narrows like the ebb and flow of the tides. The one with the wood that glows like a coal on a fireplace grate. The one that has inlaid on the face, where the violin swells to the fullest point, a bear. A dancing bear.

Alexandra Siy

NEW TOWN

A vintage blue car parked on burnt concrete. Not the usual slick album cover. *Buena Vista Social Club* sounds more like a place than the name of a band. Three dollars used, worth a listen. I snap the disc into my Walkman and leave the record shop.

Guitars and congas. Funky old men singing in Spanish. I'm one of the blurry girls on the album, strolling in sunshine and shadows down a sizzling city street.

Okay, my out-of-body experience isn't that literal. But I am addicted to music. Like Gus is to pot.

Track 4. Piano. No singing. Just piano and some congas and, near the end, trumpet and bass solos. I listen again. It stays in my head like a theme song from a movie.

When I get home, I use my mother's credit card

to order the music from *sheetmusicplus.com* (she won't even notice). I click "Express shipping."

I'd die without the piano. Not suicidal die, but go mental die. I mean, how else could I survive living with Gus? Mean Gus. Violent Gus. My awful twin brother Gus.

Sometimes I hate him, sometimes I just feel sorry. Most of the time I'm numb. Indifference is my only weapon.

I can't stand my parents. Why won't they do something? They act baffled. (We-treated-them-equally.)

It's true, Gus and I both started piano lessons when we were eight. Gus was better, memorizing "Für Elise" before me. But by the time we got to the "Maple Leaf Rag," he'd had enough of the piano. I quit lessons last year, collateral damage in the War with Gus.

The *Buena Vista Social Club* piano book arrives FedEx in a white bubble-wrap-padded mailer. I open to page 37, "Pueblo Nuevo."

Silence. It starts with an eighth-note rest. The house is quiet, too, but I know they're hiding in their bunkers.

The C scale follows.

Do-re-mi-fa-so-la-ti! Just like in *The Sound of Music.*

Easy. I can do this.

But I can't even get through the second measure. I start over, *The Sound of Music* again.

I make it to the second line—accidentals,

triplets, how's this supposed to sound? I click on the stereo and turn up the volume.

I follow along, stalling and starting, a bad driver in the vintage blue car.

Time stops when I no longer see the notes on the staff. Then I'm inside the music, like it's a story. Things happen around me—doors slam, people argue—and I don't notice until the very end, when the chaos crescendos above the music, breaking the spell.

Mom is yelling. Dad is rubbing his forehead. Gus grabs the remote and shuts down the stereo.

My blue car brakes to a screeching halt; I duck, dodging a missile. The remote ricochets off the piano and cracks open, spilling its wires and battery onto the carpet.

In bed, I listen to Mom and Dad discuss battle plans. (We'll-send-him-away.)

Gus overhears, too; he gets up and kicks in his closet door.

▪▪▪▪

Nine pages long, "Pueblo Nuevo" is more unfamiliar than difficult. Like at the top of the piece, it says "Moderate Danzón." What's "Danzón"?

Whatever it is, I think I'm doing it, because I'm right with Rubén González, the old guy playing on the record. My fingers touch the keys and the music flows out of me and into me like a river.

It's been three weeks, and finally I'm getting it.

One, two, and three, four, and . . .

I close my eyes and play from memory. G to G,

my fingers dance along, five bars of sixteenth notes. A smile.

I'm driving the old car with bad brakes and no seat belts out of the war zone, cruising now toward a brand-new town. Until I crash.

The piano case smashes down as I snatch my fingers away. Just in time.

"Didn't you hear me?" Gus shouts. "I said, 'Shut up!'"

I can't even look at him. I never look at him anymore, the pathetic creep.

▪▪▪▪

The piano is gone. It's disappeared from its seedy nook between the bookcase and the plants.

I'll die without the piano. Not suicidal die, but go insane die. Go crazy, like Gus.

I think back to us, me and Gus. We were seven years old when he burned down our fort. He said the flames looked beautiful. So I glance out the window for black smoke billowing from a charred wooden skeleton. But the rusting swing set stands alone, its pair of chain-link swings quivering together in the wind.

Gus now—sixteen, stoned. I open the garage and check the driveway for the muddy tire prints of a truck that takes away old pianos for a roll of twenties (Gus could use those). The pavement is clean.

Gus, gone. I race around the house to the back door, where his pockmarked Jetta is pulled up against the vinyl siding. A winch is bolted to the bumper, connected to a steel cable that's threaded through the door. I'm not even a little bit amazed, because Gus knows how to do these impossible, mechanical kinds of things. Like moving the piano into the basement all by himself with a come-along and a car, and his wiry back and his whacked-out, weirdly wired brain.

I grab the wire. Its greasy tension leads me to the basement stairs. *The Sound of Music* leaks from near darkness. *Do-re-mi-fa-so-la-ti!*

Again Gus plays it, like a worn-out starter turning over and over. He sits at the piano, its dented mahogany case elegant in the narrow sunbeam that flickers through the basement window.

"Why?"

It's all I can manage, but it's enough because he turns his head and looks at me, and I see him now like it's for the first time ever. I see his fierce blue eyes beneath his black bangs, blazing from his furrowed baby face that tells me nothing. I want to lunge at him, tackle him, shout in his face, pound him until he answers me. Why?

But I am paralyzed in my sack, greedily clinging to my placenta, my piano.

Gus removes the cable from the piano frame and goes upstairs. I hear the back door close and his car engine start, and he's going to wherever he goes.

I slide onto the empty bench and play.

"Do I have to go to piano?" Gail poked at her sodden cornflakes.

"Yes." Dad's voice came from behind his newspaper.

Gail sighed, hoping her airborne discontent would float over the paper stockade.

Brian was tearing his toast into pieces and staring at the outside of Dad's paper. "What's 'Cub-ban'?" he said.

"*Kew*ban," said Dad. "Cuba is an island in the West Indies, near Florida."

"Da-ad." Gail let her spoon clatter into her bowl. "Colleen phoned. They're going to Pitt Lake today, to the farm. They invited me to come."

The voice beyond the wall was silent.

"October two-seven, one-nine-six-two." Brian

continued reading. "Cuban Missile Crisis." He finger-flicked a corner of toast at Gail. "Toast missile, kapow!"

Gail ate the missile. She spoke quietly to her cereal. "They've got goats at the farm now."

"Voodoo jet in-ter-cep-tors." Brian was getting very good at sounding out. "What's voodoo? Is there going to be a war? Have they got lots of bombs?"

The kitchen door swung open as Brian continued his volley of questions. Mum stood in the doorway. She had her coat on. "There is most definitely not going to be a war."

"Rats," said Brian. "I love bombs. *Pafoom! Pafoom!*"

Dad peered over the top of his paper. "I don't know, Wilma. Khrushchev is saying . . ."

Mum poured a mug of coffee. "Brian, be quiet." She ran a glug of cold water into the mug. "There won't be a war, because Russia and the United States are both members of the United Nations, for Pete's sake."

More of Dad appeared over the paper. "You trust Khrushchev? And Castro?"

"Peeeow, peeeow." Brian had a piece of sausage on his fork and was machine-gunning his toast. *"Ack-ack, ack-ack-ack."*

"Stop that, Brian. But if we don't place our faith in the UN, then we're just back in the old game."

Brian stepped up the volume and frequency of his sausage attack.

"Brian!" Mum grabbed Brian's wrist. "What did I tell you? Stop that noise!"

"Owwww, you're hurting me!" Brian tore his arm away and ran to the door of the kitchen. "And anyway, I'm not going to be a stupid old pirate on Halloween. You can't make me. I'm going to be a juvenile delinquent." He fled, slamming the door behind him.

Gail waited for her parents to grin at each other. Brian had a passionate ambition to be a juvenile delinquent, which to him meant riding his bicycle very fast while yelling, "Yeah? You and who else?" It was funny in that six-year-old-boy kind of way. Mum and Dad used to find it funny, anyway. They used to look at each other over his head and their lips would twitch, and then one or the other would glance at Gail, including her. But it had been a long time since the family had been linked by jokes or glances.

The noise of the slam echoed in the air. Dad lowered his paper to the table. "Wilma?"

Mum gulped her coffee. "The bus. I'm opening today, so I can't be late."

"I could drive you."

"No. It's my job and my schedule. Stop rescuing me."

Mum exploded out the back door. Gail glanced up from under her eyebrows and saw Dad recoil and shrink. She wanted to hit him. Parents have no right to look like that—wounded.

"So, do I have to go to piano?"

Dad got up and began clearing the table. "Of course."

Gail pushed her chair back. It gave a satisfying squeal across the linoleum. "Why?" It wasn't quite a whine, but she did turn the word into two syllables.

Dad turned to her. "Two reasons, Gail. Commitment and responsibility."

There was no answer to this except silence. Parents always win.

▪▪▪▪

Gail trudged down the hill toward Mrs. G's apartment building. She held her music case in front of her and bashed it with her knees, making it bounce. Her left knee was commitment and her right knee was responsibility. Right about now Colleen's family would be leaving for the farm, all the kids in the back of the station wagon. When they horsed around, Colleen's mother would pretend to be mean and say, "Any more of that noise and I'm dumping you all off the Pitt River Bridge." Then all the kids would pretend to be afraid.

Gail's family used to have pretends. Dad would be a human vacuum and chase Brian and her around the house. Mum could do a perfect imitation of Miss Cope at the post office. Miss Cope was freshly surprised by each new customer. "What's this? A letter! Well, fancy that!" A good group pretend happened last Christmas. Gail got a hula hoop and all four of them squished together to fit inside the bright green plastic ring, an eight-legged hula-hooping octopus.

But now Mum had turned into a yeller and Dad was silent. Gail did her best to bring everybody back inside the hula hoop. She tried being Miss Cope at dinner. "What do we have here? A carrot? My goodness, you could knock me down with a feather!" But nobody noticed.

Gail's knees were starting to smart from being battered. She allowed herself to stop as she reached Mrs. G's apartment building. Joanie Snowden, who had the lesson before her, was just coming out the door. A little presto-run up the stairs and Gail would be right on time.

■■■■

Three sharps, A major. Scales in similar and contrary motion. Three sharps were two sharps too many. Gail's brain and fingers fumbled, and the piano fought back. But Mrs. G didn't correct her. Staring off into the distance, she didn't seem to notice.

Gail opened up *Piano Round the Year.* "Should I play my piece now?"

Mrs. G nodded. "Go ahead."

Gail turned to "Halloween Pranks" while stealing glimpses at Mrs. G. What was up? Usually she was full of gentle suggestions, conversation, and stories. The stories were often about being a newcomer. Last week, for example, she had talked about her first Canadian Halloween. "The doorbell rings one evening and here are ghosts and

Gypsies. They say I must give them a treat, so I invite them in and give them tea and strudel. Then I play Chopin for them. I think Chopin is always a treat, *ja?*"

"Halloween Pranks" was corny but easy, with no fancy stuff for the left hand. Over the week, Gail had practiced it a lot instead of practicing the A-major scale. Parents don't care what you play as long as you keep it up for twenty minutes.

▪▪▪▪

In the middle of the final repeat, Gail felt a sneeze climbing up the back of her nose. She lifted her hands from the keyboard, inhaled, and willed the tickle to explode: *"Aaaaaa . . ."*

Suddenly Mrs. G swiveled on the piano bench and engulfed Gail in a face-crushing hug. "Don't cry. Don't cry. It's all right. No bombs. Not this time."

Sheer surprise halted the sneeze. Mrs. G's watch, the one she wore pinned as a brooch to her large, soft front, was digging into Gail's cheek. She blinked. Please don't let me sneeze on Mrs. G's . . . *"CHOOO!"*

Gail kept her eyes closed, wondering about the snot content of the explosion and wondering about what time was "not this time."

Mrs. G took her gently by the shoulders and held her away at arm's length. She looked confused. "Sneezing?"

"It's the flowers," said Gail, pointing to the arrangement of dried flowers on the piano.

Mrs. G stared at her. "Sneezing, not crying." Then she began to laugh, a hiccupy sort of laugh with tears rolling down her cheeks.

Gail snuck a peek at Mrs. G's silky front. There was a damp patch, but it didn't look slimy. Mrs. G pulled a large handkerchief out of her sleeve and wiped her eyes. "We are right to sneeze and laugh and play music. No bombs. No war. Not again. Now is modern. Mr. Kennedy and Mr. Khrushchev, they talk. We have learned, *ja?*"

She closed *Piano Round the Year.* "Today is not for lessons. Today we have a concert." She gestured to the fat brocade armchair. "Best seat for you."

Gail settled herself on the chair. Mrs. G closed all the music books and set them on top of the piano. Then, setting her fingers on the keys, she began to play.

The air stampeded with the sound of thunder and lightning dancing. Gail stared at Mrs. G's fingers, moving faster than she could see. Where next? Mrs. G was not so much playing the notes as tossing them away, throwing a double handful of water up into the sunlight.

As the music continued, Mrs. G began to disappear. Mrs. G with her dried flowers and her stories of Papa Haydn and her shiny dresses and her funny accent. All that was just a costume. The real Mrs. G was a pair of flying hands.

The music wound up tighter and tighter until the bossy left hand bashed away on some chords way down low, trying to keep everything in line.

There was a sliver of a pause, a decision; then they were all off and running again, in a fast-forward cartoon skip. The left hand could crash all it liked, but the goblins were loose. Goblin clowns with bolo bats and small tricycles and big shoes. Suddenly, like the squirt of water from a gag corsage, it came to Gail that the music was funny. Not funny peculiar or funny ha-ha but something else, strong and strange and happy in a way you didn't expect. It was a third kind of funny, like . . . when somebody thinks you are going to burst into tears and they comfort you but all you were really going to do was sneeze, but you are happy to be hugged anyway, for other reasons. For parents who don't look at each other and for eating breakfast in a kitchen where the air is about to shatter.

It was nearly done, and nearly done, and then done. Mrs. G rested her hands on the keyboard. The last chord rang in Gail's ears.

"Schubert Piano Sonata in C Minor. Final movement, the Allegro. When I was a girl, I played this piece in a competition."

"Did you learn it by heart?"

Mrs. G nodded.

"Did you win?"

Mrs. G rolled her eyes. "No. I played very badly. I had . . . *Wie sagt man das?* Stage fright, that's it. My teacher was very disappointed in me."

"But now it sounds perfect."

"Lots of practice. In the years when I did not

have a piano, I played it on the edge of a table. It was a good thing to have stored in my fingers."

"How come you didn't have a piano?"

Mrs. G was silent. Gail shifted and the plastic covering on the chair crackled.

"It was the war. Things were . . . lost. Finally, all we had was what was inside us."

The hum of street noise was cut by a *sforzando* of exploding firecrackers, followed by boy-laughter. Mrs. G jumped slightly, then shook her head. "But all of that is over. You don't want to hear sad stories. For you, the world will be in tune, *ja*? Only happy. No more wars. And you will be fine because you have it, you know. You are my most promising student."

Knock me down with a feather, thought Gail. "But what about Joanie Snowden? She's in grade-nine conservatory."

"Ah, Joanie. She works very hard." Mrs. G pointed her finger in pretend anger. "Harder than you. But with her . . . there are no surprises. But you, you have it in your fingers. All those scales I make you do? That is so it can go free one day."

She patted the seat beside her. "Come, piano four hands, and then we have tea."

▪▪▪▪

Gail loved the carpet in the hall of Mrs. G's building. Blue, brown, and green, like a map. Rivers, mountains, plains. She walked over it in her seven-league boots, striding across valleys, traversing whole countries in a single step, skipping over oceans.

When she got to the big window at the head of the stairs, she stopped and set her music case on the floor. She positioned her hands on the windowsill and began to play. Sonatina in C by M. Clementi, first movement, the Allegro. Her recital piece, learned by heart. Loud, cheerful first part with lots of runs. Quiet, moody second part with accidentals and a crescendo. It was a flawless performance. Sun streamed through the window, covering the world map in silver light. Gail rolled her left hand on the final arpeggio, gave a brief nod to acknowledge her ecstatic audience, and looked outside.

Everything was in costume. The king of the city streets on an important mission, disguised as a scruffy white dog. Bare black branches against the blue sky, playing dead, hiding the explosion of pink blossom to come. An old man with a cane, picking his way along the sidewalk, keeping secret the boy inside him—a whirling boy carrying a wizard's wand, a fishing rod, a stick to play a picket fence.

And her own hands. Gail studied them, a pair of newly encountered strangers. Grubby around the knuckles and nails bitten to the quick. A clever camouflage of ordinary kid hands. Inside, though, a key. More. Every key, major and minor. Hands just waiting to join the hard, complicated harmonies of the world.

AUTHORS' NOTES

Jennifer Armstrong grew up with piano and flute lessons, and wishes she had practiced more. Her favorite piece to play on the piano now is "Get Out of Town" by Cole Porter. She also has a concertina, but it is ridiculously baffling to learn how to play. This is the second collection of short stories she has edited. For more about her books, see her Web site at *www.jennifer-armstrong.com.*

Ibtisam S. Barakat writes: "I love to sing. When I was growing up in Ramallah, I first tried to learn bird songs—cardinals, robins, roosters. I practiced till Mother called me in. Later, I memorized radio songs. I stood on a hill outside, closed my eyes, swayed like a ribbon in the wind, and sang into a bunch of poppy flowers. As a writer, I think music is the water of writing; words are grains, the flour.

Together, with the longing to feed the world words that nourish, and lots of pounding at the pages, writers make magic bread for the mind." You can reach her at *i_barakat@yahoo.com.*

Joseph Bruchac's work as a writer, storyteller, and occasional performer of traditional Native American music often reflects his Abenaki Indian heritage and his lifetime connection to the Adirondack region of New York State.

Sarah Ellis grew up in Vancouver, Canada, and was a serious violin student at age six, but she's been going musically downhill ever since. Nowadays, writing takes up most of her time, with fiction and picture books for children, book reviews, and presentations on children's literature. Her most recent book is *The Several Lives of Orphan Jack,* published by Groundwood Books. When she gets a minute, though, she is definitely going to learn a fourth chord on her ukulele.

Gail Giles lives and writes in Fairbanks, Alaska. She plays the guitar but says, "My husband and pets would rather I watercolor, read, or sleep than play the guitar. And they never allow me to sing." You can visit her at *www.gailgiles.com.*

J. Alison James has been writing and translating books for children since 1990, when her first novel, *Sing for a Gentle Rain,* came out. She lives in northern Vermont but considers herself an international citizen, as she has lived in or visited more countries than she can remember. She grew up playing the flute, and now her daughters play violin and cello. Her house is filled with music.

Ron Koertge is sixty-three, a former teacher at Pasadena City College in Southern California, a full-time fiction writer, and a part-time handicapper of Thoroughbred horses. His latest novels for teenagers are *Stoner & Spaz* (winner of the 2003 PEN Center USA Literary Award for Children's Literature) and *Shakespeare Bats Cleanup,* a novel in verse. His latest book of poems is *Geography of the Forehead* (University of Arkansas Press), and his latest handicapping triumph was a horse that paid $53 after everybody else said it didn't have a chance.

David Levithan took guitar lessons for two years in elementary school, mostly so he could copy down the lyrics of his favorite songs from the sheet music at the front of the music store. He hasn't attempted to play an instrument since. But he has played his stereo (sometimes quite loud) for most of his life. He and his friend Dawn have exchanged mixes every month for the past nine years. He's also written books that are full of references to his favorite singers and songs, most recently *Boy Meets Boy* and *The Realm of Possibility.*

Jude Mandell writes: "'Prodigy' is based on my own life, altered for dramatic impact. Don't look for my albums, though. I wasn't a famous diva, although I performed professionally in musicals, opera, even Second City children's theater. *The Children's Hour* was a real show. It aired first on radio and then on TV, helping performers such as Eddie Fisher and Frankie Avalon reach stardom. I was on the show for three years. When the story about my sister and me began to hum inside my head, it pulsed like a ballad. After many years, I've finally found the courage to let our story step onto a page and sing." You can visit Jude at *www.judemandell.com.*

Ann Manheimer says: "After being kicked out of my elementary school chorus, I didn't think music would be a big part of my life. That changed when I was a teenager, when songs from the civil rights movement and musicians like Pete Seeger inspired me to pick up a guitar and sing. Later, a good-looking guitar player taught me about blues and rock. Now our daughters keep my ears current. Whatever the era or genre, music matters." Ann Manheimer lives in California.

Dian Curtis Regan says: "Cora's explanation of synesthesia as a 'cross-wiring of sensory areas in the brain' is a simple way of saying that synesthesia means 'joined senses'—two, or even all five, senses respond at the same time to what a person sees, hears, smells, tastes, or feels. This condition is the opposite of *anesthesia,* which means 'no sensation.'"

While researching this story, Dian was surprised by the number of friends who told her they had synesthesia and realized that she, too, has a mild form of "time synesthesia."

Dian is the author of forty books for young readers, ranging from picture books *(Chance)* to middle grade fiction *(Monster of the Month Club)* to young adult novels *(Princess Nevermore)*. Her short stories have appeared in anthologies such as *Shattered, Soul Searching, Dirty Laundry,* and *Period Pieces.* Dian, a native of Colorado, has also lived in Texas, Oklahoma, and Venezuela. Presently she lives in Kansas. Her Web site is *www.diancurtisregan.com.*

Alexandra Siy writes: "In third grade I started piano lessons as well as violin, and later played cello and viola in my high school orchestra—I loved 'Hoe-Down' from Copland's *Rodeo* and Bach's *Brandenburg Concertos.* But at home I listened to rock and roll and played the piano, mainly Beatles tunes: 'Hey Jude,' 'Lady Madonna,' 'The Long and Winding Road.' . . . Anyway, music helped me survive adolescence in a really messed-up family. About twenty years later, in 1997, Ry Cooder, producer of the *Buena Vista Social Club* recording, wrote, 'In Cuba the music . . . takes care of you and rebuilds you from the inside out.' That 'refined and deeply funky' sound, as Cooder puts it, got inside of me and inspired this story. I'm grateful to all the

musicians on the record, especially the late pianist Rubén González (1919–2003); and Jennifer Armstrong for including 'New Town' in this book."
Alexandra Siy *(www.alexandrasiy.com)* lives in New York with her husband and children, where she writes, listens to music, and occasionally plays the piano.